"Are you okay?" Stone asked.

"I— Yes." Felicity didn't have time to explain to him why avalanches were her worst nightmare. Not when there was work to be done.

Tugger whined and pressed against her leg as he'd been taught to do as a therapy dog. She reached out and absently ran a hand between Tugger's ears to steady her insides.

She could cry into her pillow tonight when she was alone and the people of Holden Springs were safe.

"I'll take Tugger and Dandy with me," she said, referring to the pit bull at her side and a young black Labrador retriever who was part of the therapy-dog program.

"I can tag along, if there's anything I can do to assist," Stone said. "That way you'll have an extra person for the dogs."

The last thing she needed was Stone alongside her. It would distract her from her real work.

She sighed deeply.

A bruised ankle.

Stone's unnerving presence.

And now an avalanche.

Could things *get* any worse?

A *Publishers Weekly* bestselling and award-winning author of over forty novels, **Deb Kastner** lives in beautiful Colorado with her husband, miscreant mutts and curious kitties. She is blessed with three adult daughters and two grandchildren. Her favorite hobby is spoiling her grandchildren, but she also enjoys reading, watching movies, listening to music—The Texas Tenors are her favorite— singing in the church choir and exploring the Rocky Mountains on horseback.

Books by Deb Kastner

Love Inspired

Rocky Mountain Family

The Black Sheep's Salvation
Opening Her Heart
The Marine's Mission
Their Unbreakable Bond

Cowboy Country

Yuletide Baby
The Cowboy's Forever Family
The Cowboy's Surprise Baby
The Cowboy's Twins
Mistletoe Daddy
The Cowboy's Baby Blessing
And Cowboy Makes Three
A Christmas Baby for the Cowboy
Her Forgotten Cowboy

Visit the Author Profile page at LoveInspired.com for more titles.

Their Unbreakable Bond

Deb Kastner

LOVE INSPIRED

INSPIRATIONAL ROMANCE

LOVE INSPIRED®
INSPIRATIONAL ROMANCE

ISBN-13: 978-1-335-56744-4

Their Unbreakable Bond

Copyright © 2021 by Debra Kastner

This edition published by arrangement with Harlequin Books S.A.

For questions and comments about the quality of this book, please contact us at CustomerService@Harlequin.com.

Love Inspired
22 Adelaide St. West, 40th Floor
Toronto, Ontario M5H 4E3, Canada
www.LoveInspired.com

Printed in U.S.A.

Yea, though I walk through the valley of the shadow of death, I will fear no evil: for thou art with me; thy rod and thy staff they comfort me.
—*Psalm* 23:4

To my father, who has taught me more about life than I can ever express. Dad, I watched you work hard for your family every day. Protecting and providing for us without a word of complaint no matter how hard it got was always front and center for you and I'm grateful for it.

You showed me what love and commitment really means, and I don't think it's any big surprise that all three of your children married once for life. I remember when you had to go work on an oil rig for several months and the moment you returned you rushed to Mom and embraced her with all the love in your heart.

You were also the one who first created in me a love of reading. You held me on your lap as a young child and sang and read to me. You kept your books where I could easily find them, and it was through you I learned the wonders of reading.

I love you, Dad!

Chapter One

It was the Be Back Shortly sign on the door of the gift shop, with an arrow pointing toward the barn, that had sent Stone Keller in this direction. And he'd stopped on spotting a brown-and-white pit bull mix worriedly pacing and barking in front of the open door of an aluminum-sided shed located on the side of the barn.

Stone was starting work today at the Christmas Tree Farm at Winslow's Woodlands, and he was in search of his best friend Sharpe Winslow's baby sister Felicity, whom he was supposed to shadow in the gift shop.

If he wasn't mistaken, he'd just found her—only she wasn't in the gift shop. Nor was she in the barn.

"Felicity?" he called out, approaching the

shed, which was stuffed full of bins and boxes of various sizes and shapes, marked Christmas, Winterfest, Spring and Summer, stacked four and five high in a random manner.

"I'm okay," came a small squeak from deep inside the shed.

Maybe she was, but her response had been little more than a yelp, so Stone jogged forward and started removing boxes from the entrance to the shed, taking care but moving as fast as he was able. From the sound of her voice, he could tell she was somewhere in the deepest, darkest corner of the shed.

"Felicity? Where are you?"

"Back here." She held up one hand and waved. He could barely see her over the top of the row of bins.

"Hold on a sec and I'll get you out," he called.

"Oh, no need," she protested. "I got myself in here. I'll get myself out."

He begged to differ, though he didn't say so aloud. Rather, he continued moving boxes out into the open so he could home in on the sound of her voice.

Finally, he moved a box to reveal her face,

her cheeks a bright pink and her expression sheepish.

Except Felicity didn't look anything like he'd expected her to. Nothing at all, as a matter of fact. There was no doubt she was definitely a Winslow. She had the same high cheekbones as he remembered all three of her older sisters had. The smile lines at the corners of her eyes and the dimple in her chin were a dead ringer for the rest of her siblings, both brothers and sisters.

But Felicity—the Felicity *he* remembered, anyway, and for some reason had half expected to see—was definitely not the pretty woman staring back at him. The impish grin was the same one he recalled from her youth, but she wasn't Sharpe's annoying, bratty little sister anymore, the gawky, skinny teenage girl who used to furtively follow Stone and Sharpe around.

She'd grown up.

Well, duh. Of course she had.

He certainly was nothing like the reckless, hotheaded teenager who'd left Whispering Pines twelve years ago. It just hadn't occurred to him that Felicity would have grown into such a lovely woman.

His gut tightened. Felicity Winslow was stunning when color rose to her cheeks. Who knew the little bean he remembered from his youth would sprout into such a beautiful flower? Blond hair pulled back in a ponytail and tucked through a ball cap. Blue eyes that glittered with pride and maybe a little embarrassment.

He swallowed hard against the sudden lump in his throat and took a mental step backward even as he tipped his dark brown cowboy hat in greeting.

Felicity was his best friend's baby sister.

Well, not *baby* sister, exactly.

"Hey, Felicity. I'm—"

"Stone Keller," she finished for him, her eyes widening. "I don't believe it. What are you doing here?"

"Sharpe didn't tell you I was coming?"

Her eyebrows lowered as she scrunched her nose. She was clearly confused by his presence.

"Why?"

Her abrupt question surprised him. He'd have to have a word with Sharpe for leaving Felicity in the dark. "He's hired me for the season, or at least for as long as my mom's chemo sessions last. I moved back to town to support her. I really appreciate the opportunity to work here again."

He'd worked at the farm for a short time as a teenager before rodeo got the best of him—and the worst of him.

"That's really thoughtful of you to support your mom this way. I was so sorry to hear about her. Cancer is awful." Felicity leaned her forearms on the box in front of her, but it was unstable, and she immediately straightened. "I was sorry to hear about you, too. You just got out of the hospital after wrecking your bike, didn't you?"

Heat rose to his face, and he scrubbed a hand across his stubbled chin. The sound made the pit bull stare up at him inquisitively, although he—or was it she?—didn't appear ferocious. Just curious.

Stone knew it was too much to hope that people hadn't heard about his reckless motorcycle accident. Not in a small town like Whispering Pines, Colorado, where gossip ran rife in the best of times. For a rodeo star like he used to be, there was no chance whatsoever of sneaking into town unnoticed. He'd been one of their local heroes and was often on the lips of the gossips around Whispering Pines. Too bad he couldn't have hurt himself under a horse's hooves instead of doing something as foolish as showing off while he was motorbiking with friends on an unmarked mountain trail.

He nodded in response and sought to get out from under Felicity's frank perusal by turning the subject back to her.

"So, Sharpe told me I ought to shadow you for the day to learn what you do in the gift shop."

"Because?"

"Because I'm supposed to help?" he suggested. "He said you were busier than anyone else during this time of year when you're putting Christmas away and decorating for Winterfest."

She scoffed. "Well, that's the truth. Next to our Christmas and spring planting seasons, Winterfest is our busiest time of year. Although I have to say I'm surprised Sharpe noticed, much less admitted it to you."

Stone leaned in, trying to better assess where she was located amongst the bins and boxes. "Can you crawl out now, or would you like me to move a few more of these bins out first?"

Felicity released a long, frustrated sigh and the dog started barking.

"Hush, Tugger," she said with a frown. "My foot is stuck under one of these boxes. I was trying to dislodge it when you came along. So I guess I need you to keep coming toward me."

"Okay. It's a good thing I showed up when I did, then. You would have been stuck in there forever. Or at least until you didn't show up for dinner." He chuckled. "I'll keep digging."

He followed his words with action, moving box after box out of the way. "How did you even get back there?" he asked. He would have thought that if she were looking for a bin near the back, she would have gone about getting it another way. Something more sensible. What had she done? Crawled over the boxes to get to the back?

She huffed in exasperation. He didn't know if it was aimed at him or if she was frustrated with herself. Or maybe the sound was aimed at Tugger, who hadn't stopped barking in alarm despite her calling him off more than once.

"If you must know, I crawled over the top of the bins."

He raised his eyebrows. As far as he could tell, Felicity was a tiny thing, but crawling over boxes was in his mind a foolish way to go about getting what she needed.

"All the ones back here are full of Winterfest decorations and will need to be unloaded sometime soon, but I was looking for one set of trimmings in particular and knew they were in a bin back here. I took a shortcut to getting it. Or at least, I *tried* taking a shortcut. It was a good idea until it wasn't."

He tried to stifle his laughter and failed. She was just too cute, stuck in the dark shadows of the shed.

"Hold on," he encouraged her, pinching his lips together to hide his amusement. "I've almost got you now."

How could this be happening?

If only Tugger hadn't been such a constant companion, Stone never would have been able to locate her. The dog hadn't left her side for a moment, and she knew it was his warning bark that had brought Stone to find her.

Humiliation hummed through Felicity, making every nerve ending in her body snap with annoyance. Of all the scenarios she could have possibly imagined, Stone Keller waltzing into her life, especially given her current set of circumstances, was the outside of enough. Was it any wonder that she wanted to slink down between the boxes and hope he would go away and leave her alone in her misery? She'd rather be stuck in the shed until nightfall than have had him find her here.

But no. Stone was hard at work tossing bin after bin away from the opening to get to her. To *rescue* her. And if she wasn't mistaken, he was doing everything in his power to keep a sly grin off his face. She had no doubt he was laughing at her on the inside, even if his jaw was clamped shut to hide his amusement.

The next time she saw her brother Sharpe, she was going to verbally skin him alive. He hadn't said a single thing to her about Stone even being in town, much less coming to the farm.

Stone Keller was here to shadow her? To work with her?

It would have been nice to have been forewarned—to be forearmed, so to speak—although even without her current frame of mind, being face-to-face with Stone would have been a major issue for her.

Because Stone Keller had been her middle school crush.

It may have been years since she'd seen him, and he'd changed some physically, but even so, she would have known him anywhere. Tall, with dark red-gold hair and twinkling light blue eyes, he still carried the easy masculine confidence that had attracted her back then, although his face now showed the wear and tear of years of hard living. She'd known what kind of man he'd become, a tough cowboy and an even harder partier.

She'd followed his rodeo career until his career-ending motorcycle accident, and couldn't imagine how horrible that must have been for him. Rodeo had been his life. He was no longer a lanky cowboy whose body was made for riding on the back of a bareback horse. During his time in the hospital, possibly in physical therapy, he had clearly hit the weight room and had packed on pounds of muscle.

Even after all these years, butterflies fluttered in her stomach and sent her head spinning when she saw him. She was long past the days of teenage angst, when she'd spent hours lying on her bed staring at the ceiling, listening to love songs and dreaming of Stone Keller suddenly falling in love with her. Felicity and her friends had all lived for catching glimpses of him hanging out with her brother, though he never would have thought to speak to her. He probably hadn't even known she existed back then.

She was no longer a silly, giggly teenager, but she definitely felt something when Stone's gaze met hers and his mouth turned up at one corner—emotions she hadn't experienced in a long while and didn't dare put a name to.

It was all she could do not to fan her flaming face with her hand.

"I'm almost there," Stone assured her. "We'll have you out in no time."

She once again attempted to pull her foot loose, gritting her teeth and yanking as hard as she could, but the boxes had shifted around her ankle and she was stuck even tighter than before, giving her no other choice than to accept Stone's help.

"Here we go." He'd finally found her. He carefully lifted off the bins binding her foot, which were stacked four high in every direction. Tugger wiggled his way in and licked her face, clearly relieved that he could now reach her.

She couldn't help but wince when her ankle was suddenly free from the weight of the boxes. She gritted her teeth when pain suddenly radiated up her leg.

Stone frowned and stepped forward, wrapping one arm securely around her waist and offering his other for support. "Here. Sit down and let's take a look at this ankle."

It was bad enough that she'd put herself in this situation in the first place, but it was even worse that she was distracted more by the touch of his fingers than from the pain in her ankle. She hopped on her good foot, hoping to be able to stand on her own, but she quickly discovered she was unable to put any pressure on her bad ankle without it throbbing in discomfort.

"Please. We need to get you seated." He

slowly and tenderly helped her sit on top of a sturdy nearby bin and dropped to one knee, reaching for her foot. "Don't move. Let me check it out first."

For someone with hands as large and rough as his, he was surprisingly gentle when he touched her, slowly pressing the area around her anklebone with his fingers and feeling for any obvious wounds.

She was determined to not make a big deal out of this no matter how bad her ankle actually was. She was already so embarrassed she was certain her face was cherry red. But when Stone brushed his fingers over the outside of her anklebone, she couldn't help but let out a small whimper of distress.

"Did you twist your foot when the bin fell on it?" he asked in the raspy tone she remembered so well. His voice had deepened since she'd seen him last, but his husky tone was still there, probably from the years of rodeo dust he'd swallowed along the way.

She shook her head. "No. I don't think so. I was trying to open a bin when one of the boxes fell. Its sharp edge banged my ankle and must have cut into my foot."

"Take off your shoe," he suggested, and she

suddenly wished she was wearing cowboy boots instead of the sneakers she'd thrown on that morning. Boots wouldn't just have better protected her foot, but Stone wouldn't be pulling it off as he was with her sneaker.

He rolled off her sock and leaned in, squinting to see her foot.

"It's too dark in here. We'll be better able to see things once I've gotten you out of the shed and into the daylight, but you have a good-sized bruise on your anklebone and the box definitely sliced your foot open."

"Nothing a bandage can't fix," she murmured.

He half shrugged. "Maybe. Let's first get you out of this shed."

Without waiting, he scooped her into his arms and strode out the door of the shed.

How many times had Felicity imagined this very thing as a teenager? And now here she was, really truly in Stone's arms and wishing she were anywhere but here.

"Please…let me down," she pleaded through clenched teeth, as much from the humiliation as from the pain.

He set her down on the grass and plunked down next to her, his gaze on her foot, which

Felicity had almost completely forgotten about for a moment there. Tugger dashed back and forth barking frenetically, probably reacting to Stone's nervous energy.

"It's not so bad," she assured Stone, squeezing her eyes shut so he couldn't see the pain in her gaze. "Really. Tugger, hush!"

He shook his head. "I'm not convinced. I see a little blood here, and I'm not qualified to tell you if you've sprained your ankle or not. Maybe you should have a doctor take a look."

"No," she snapped, then shrugged an apology. "Sorry. I just don't want to make a bigger deal out of this than it is. You know what will happen if either of my brothers gets wind that I've done something as stupid as crawl over boxes to get inside the shed. They'll tease me mercilessly."

"Yeah, well…what are you going to do, then? Because I'm not just going to walk away from you when you're as lame as a horse with a bad shoe. Should I carry you up to the house?"

"No! Absolutely not! I can walk by myself," she assured him, although she wasn't certain that was the truth. But she was going to do it alone or make a total fool of herself trying. "Help me onto my feet, please."

"Are you sure?" He didn't look the least bit convinced.

"I banged my ankle on the corner of a box. I didn't sprain it."

"Still…"

"Can you just help me get up?" She was exasperated beyond words, more at herself than at him.

He stood and lifted her to her feet but kept one arm around her waist to steady her. "How's it feel?"

Gingerly, she put her weight on the bad ankle and grimaced. At least her leg didn't buckle underneath her. "It hurts. A little. But it will hold my weight. I've got an elastic bandage in the gift shop. I'll wrap it up."

"And you'll give me your word you'll see the doctor if it gets any worse—if it swells up or bruises, or if you have trouble walking on it."

"Yes. Okay."

"Promise?"

She didn't understand why he was pressing the issue so much. It was just an ankle, not as if she'd fallen backward and hit her head. Surely she'd know better than anyone if she needed to see the doctor? Granted, she could be stubborn about such things, but what was the point of spending money on a doctor when all the doctor would do was tell her to wrap it, ice it and elevate it? She knew to do that without having to shell out her hard-earned cash.

"Felicity?" Ruby's voice came from behind her, and she half turned to see her sister running up, flushed and out of breath.

"What's wrong?" She knew her sister well enough to know something was seriously bothering her. For one thing, Ruby loved to tease her, and here she was with Stone's arm around her waist. That was plenty to taunt her with, but Ruby appeared oblivious. Felicity straightened so Ruby wouldn't notice she'd hurt her leg.

"It's Holden Springs," Ruby puffed out, bracing her hands on her knees to catch her breath.

"What about it?" Felicity's gut churned even as the words left her lips. What had happened to the small ski town?

"There's been an avalanche. It's really bad. The last I heard, half the town has been displaced, and the number of people missing is growing by the minute."

Felicity squeezed her eyes closed against the one word that for her was the worst in the English language.

Avalanche.

Lord, anything but an avalanche.

"Are you okay?" Stone asked, tightening his hold around her waist and gripping one of her hands.

"I—yes." She didn't have time to explain to Stone why this had nothing to do with her sore ankle, nor why avalanches were her worst nightmare and that was the real reason why she'd suddenly swayed in his arms.

Not when there was work to be done. There were people in Holden Springs who needed help, and she knew she should be there.

Tugger whined and pressed against her leg as he'd been taught to do as a therapy dog. He could tell her heart rate had increased and her pulse was pounding in her ears, even if she didn't show it in her expression, although there was probably that, too. The dog was responding to cues most humans couldn't see, and Felicity reached out and absently ran a hand between Tugger's ears to steady her insides.

"Have they set up a temporary disaster shelter yet?" she asked.

"Yes. At Holden High School. They're using the cafeteria and the gym, I think. I'd go myself except I have clients in the middle of service dog training back at A New Leash on Love. Do you mind taking Tugger and heading out there?"

Felicity *did* mind. More than anyone would ever know, because she never talked about it, not even to her five siblings. But now was not the time to give in to those feelings. She could cry into her pillow later when she was alone, and the people of Holden Springs were safe.

"I'll take Tugger." She nodded. "And Dandy, too," she said, referring to a young black Labrador retriever who was part of the therapy dog program.

"I can tag along, if there's anything I can do to assist," Stone said. "That way you'll have an extra person for the dogs."

Felicity was going to decline but Ruby spoke up first. "Thank you, Stone. They need all the help they can get. From what I hear, there are a lot of families who were suddenly evacuated from their homes."

"It's settled, then," Stone said. "I'm going with you."

Felicity didn't *feel* settled. The last thing she needed was Stone alongside her. It would distract her from her real work.

She sighed deeply.

A bruised ankle.

Stone's unnerving presence.

And now an avalanche.

Could things *get* any worse?

Chapter Two

Taking Tugger with them, Stone and Felicity made a quick stop by the gift shop to wrap her ankle in a bandage before grabbing Dandy and gear for both dogs from A New Leash on Love's training facility. Soon they were heading for Holden Springs and the avalanche disaster shelter being set up at the high school. There would be a lot of work to do there for everyone involved. Stone was driving his dual-cab truck and paid close attention to the icy winter mountain roads, but his gaze often drifted to Felicity.

He'd made a couple of attempts to start a conversation as he drove, but Felicity didn't appear interested in talking. She stared out the passenger window, an unreadable expression on her face. Stone suspected her ankle must be giving her a lot more trouble than she was letting on, because something was clearly bothering her. He admired her grit, but her stoicism was unnecessary, and he wished she'd just talk to him about it.

"Are you going to be okay?" he asked as he pulled into the parking lot of Holden High School. The place was busy, with people rushing in and out of the building at a frantic pace.

Felicity turned to look at him. To his surprise, her eyes were filled with moisture.

"Yes. I'm fine," she said, wiping her palms over her eyes to stem the tears.

"You don't look fine." He didn't want to press her and make everything worse for her, but he honestly wasn't sure she should be here. "Should you even be working on that ankle of yours?"

She narrowed her gaze on him. "This isn't about me or my stupid ankle. These people need all the help we can give them. I'm here and I'm going to work no matter how I feel."

She was stubborn, but he found himself admiring that quality in her. No matter how she personally felt, the only thing on her mind was helping other people. It was a character strength from which he could learn, to be sure.

"Okay. Tell me what we're here to do. With the dogs, I mean. I understand many families have been displaced, so they're probably setting up cots in the gym, right?" He turned in his seat and leaned his forearm on the steering wheel, reaching into the back seat with his other arm to scratch a whining Dandy behind the ears.

"We'll be there to do whatever they want help with. We just need to find whoever is directing things and they'll let us know their most crucial needs, and then we and the dogs will take it from there. You'll be surprised how many ways a service animal can be useful in a situation such as this."

They unloaded the dogs, dressed them up in bright red service dog vests and made their way into the high school building. Following the directions of people in orange vests, they found the gym, where the majority of those displaced were hovering about, waiting to hear news of their friends and families, and to see what alternative housing arrangements were being made. Tugger was at Felicity's side while Stone handled Dandy, who'd morphed from excited, nearly frantic puppy into work mode the moment the red vest had been placed over him.

"We need to find whoever is in charge," Felicity reiterated, eyes scanning the gym.

Stone couldn't believe the change in her. Gone was the pensive woman who hadn't said more than a couple of words during the entire drive to Holden Springs. In her place was a strong, capable woman who knew beyond a doubt she had a reason to be there.

A couple of well-placed questions later, Felicity and Stone were approaching an orange-vested woman named Donna, who scribbled notations on the clipboard she carried, eyebrows scrunched over her nose.

"Tell us how we can help you. What's your most important need right now?" Felicity asked Donna after she and Stone had introduced themselves.

"We have trucks coming in with cots, blankets and other sundries, as well as food for the cafeteria kitchen. Everything is being unloaded in the truck entrance behind the kitchen. We need as many strong arms as we can get to have everything moved where it needs to be."

Stone was more than willing to offer his own strong arms, but he was concerned about Felicity with her bad ankle. The last thing she should be doing was lifting heavy boxes, much less walking around with them.

Felicity clearly had no such worries, or at least none that she'd voice. Stone had already learned just in this one day with her that even if her ankle was hurting, she wasn't going to say so. Complaining didn't appear to be in her vocabulary.

"This is where the plastic toboggans we loaded into your truck will come in handy," she told him. He'd wondered about that, but now it made perfect sense. They could load the toboggans and make far fewer trips with more weight on each one. He would just have to convince Felicity that she could direct things while he'd be the one to do all the carrying and pulling.

They went back to Stone's truck to unload the sleds and Felicity rooted around in a box of dog equipment she'd had him place in the back seat before they left. It didn't take her long to pull out sled harnesses for each of the dogs, and Stone realized he wasn't going to have to argue with Felicity about the pulling part where the toboggans were concerned, anyway.

She tossed one to Stone and tacked up Tugger with the other. "They'll be doing the grunt work," she explained, helping Stone to fit Dandy with his harness.

"Good idea. I never would have thought of that."

"This isn't my first rodeo, cowboy." She smiled at him, although it didn't quite reach her eyes, which still made Stone feel as if she was in some kind of pain she wasn't voicing.

Before long, they were pulling boxes out of rental trucks and stacking them onto the toboggans that the dogs hauled to the truck entrance behind the cafeteria, where others helped unload the sleds. Felicity had gone quiet as she worked. He could tell she was clenching her jaw and her shoulders were tight. As far as he could tell, she wasn't limping, but he thought maybe she was consciously thinking about every step she took.

Whatever was bothering her, it didn't stop her from slinging boxes onto and off the toboggans at a steady pace. Stone had wondered how well Tugger and Dandy would work with the toboggans, but clearly both of the dogs had done some pulling in the past. They were obviously well trained, and they listened to Felicity's commands intently.

"Did you teach them how to do this?" he asked, trying to pull Felicity's mind away from the pain in her ankle.

"Yes. All four of us Winslow girls participate in the training our dogs get. We teach many of our larger dogs how to pull wagons and toboggans. You'd be surprised how often that comes in handy in one way or another."

"I can imagine." Despite the fact that it was a brisk twenty degrees outside and the wind was blowing, Stone had broken out into a sweat. He lifted his cowboy hat and brushed his sleeve across his forehead, even while noticing Felicity's bright pink cheeks, her unusually shiny eyes, and the cloudy puffs emerging from her mouth as she gasped for breath.

"The trucks are almost all unloaded. Do you want to take a quick break to go inside and get warm?" he suggested. "Then afterward we can find something else to do to help," he added, knowing that would be first on Felicity's mind, even over her own discomfort.

After a moment's thought, she nodded, and they unhooked the dogs from the toboggans and threw the sleds in the back of Stone's truck before making their way inside. In the gym, cots were being set up for the people huddled around the room, all of whom looked miserable. Even though most of them kept to a low murmur, Stone couldn't help but notice the noise level in the gym.

"This is frightening," he said as he watched a young mother attempting to hush her frightened, screaming baby to no avail. "These poor people, to be displaced this way all of the sudden. It's a good reminder that things can change in the blink of an eye. You just never know from moment to moment."

Only then did he glance toward Felicity. For the second time that day, her eyes were illuminated by the hint of tears, though none fell down her cheeks. She was obviously a woman who felt deeply and wasn't afraid to show her emotions. She had a soft heart that Stone greatly admired. She was in distress, but it didn't keep her from being here. She'd been the one to step forward when Ruby told them of the avalanche. Her injured ankle hadn't stopped her at all.

He immediately regretted having made the comment about the suffering families around them. He hadn't meant to call attention to the obvious, especially since it had clearly upset Felicity so much.

"Hey," he said, reaching for her hand. "This is all new to me, but I didn't mean to upset you."

"No. I know," she said raggedly. "You didn't. I feel the same way when I see all that these people have been through. This is tough for everyone. Let's go see if there's something else we can do to help."

She hadn't even taken a five-minute break before she was already raring to get back into the middle of things.

"I can go look for Donna and find out what needs to be done next," he offered. "Why don't you just sit there and rest that ankle for a while longer."

She speared him with her gaze. "I didn't come here to sit around. Besides, I'm the one who knows how best to use the dogs. Let's find Donna together."

He shook his head. Her determination was astonishing, and it made him step it up a notch. This woman was not only strong, but she was good for him in the best possible ways.

He felt as if in meeting Felicity—or rather, getting to know her—he had just stepped into a whole other world.

He just hoped he was ready to meet the challenge.

Within five minutes, they'd checked in with Donna and were told most of the cots had already been set up. The next big chore would be to start passing out bottles of water to make sure everyone stayed hydrated.

"This is the perfect job for us," Felicity told Stone as he pulled a red children's wagon full of cases of water. "While we pass out water we can talk to people and comfort them, and the best part is, the dogs can do their thing."

"Do what thing?"

"You'll see. They instinctively know how to make people feel better. Tugger and Dandy in particular have been trained to respond to physical symptoms that suggest stress. And they're especially great with kids."

They decided to start in the far corner and slowly work their way down the aisles so they wouldn't miss anyone.

Felicity focused all her energy on concentrating on those around her, but two things were stopping her—and neither one was the pain in her ankle, which she was actually grateful for, because the throbbing helped keep her mind off memories of Trevor's death and the unnerving feeling of having Stone by her side. It didn't help that he hovered over her, worrying about her.

Of course he didn't know her history. But his actions were enough to motivate her to set aside her emotions, locking them away in her heart.

"Let me show you something remarkable," she told Stone as he handed water bottles to a young family who'd pushed their cots together to make more room for others. Their two small daughters—Felicity guessed their ages were around four and two—were sitting on the edge of one cot, clinging to their dollies and looking around the room with large, confused eyes.

"Hi, there," Felicity said, approaching the mother, who had her arms wrapped around the younger of the two dark-haired girls. "I'm Felicity and this is Stone, and we're here to provide water for your family."

"I'm Jason," the father said, his voice tight with strain as he reached out and shook Felicity's hand, then Stone's. Felicity could only imagine the pressure he was under, trying to care for his displaced family. "This is my wife, Mariella, and our daughters, Ariana and Lily."

"It's nice to meet you, although I'm sorry for the circumstances." Felicity glanced at Stone and they shared a moment of compassion for this family. She was praying nonstop in her heart and suspected Stone was, as well.

Felicity called Tugger forward and commanded him to sit, which he immediately and eagerly did. Felicity could read from Tugger's expression that he knew his job and was more than ready to do his part to make this family feel better.

"This is Tugger, and he loves to make new friends. He has a special fondness for little girls. Would it be okay for your daughters to pet him?"

Ariana squeaked in excitement while Lily's eyes noticeably widened.

"He's friendly?" Jason asked even as Mariella smiled and nodded her assent, reaching out her own hand to stroke Tugger's neck.

It wasn't the first time Felicity had been questioned about Tugger, but she didn't take offense to the query. It wasn't really all that surprising that people would ask, given that he was a pit bull mix. There was a lot of misinformation floating around about the breed, and Tugger was a wonderful ambassador to demonstrate the truth. There wasn't a kinder, gentler dog of *any* breed in Colorado.

And he especially loved children.

"Tugger is the friendliest dog in our service program," she assured Jason, who then reached out to scratch the pit bull behind his ears before he gave his okay to his girls. He laughed when Tugger's ear-to-ear pit bull smile appeared and he cocked his head, his tongue lolling out to one side.

"Go ahead, girls," Jason said with a chuckle. "It appears he really is friendly."

Once again, Tugger had won them over, just as Felicity knew he would.

The older of the two girls flung her arms around Tugger's neck. Her sudden movement may have startled another dog, but not Tugger, who was a trained therapy dog through and through. If anything, he leaned into the girl, begging for more attention and hugs.

It wasn't too much longer before Lily lost her reticence and also gave Tugger a big hug. In sheer doggy happiness, Tugger wagged his tail like a circular fan, round and round, so fast it was surprising he didn't lift off the ground.

Stone chuckled, lightening the mood in this small corner of the room. Felicity knew how he felt. She remembered the first time she'd worked in a disaster relief shelter. If she hadn't seen it for herself, she never would have believed what a difference a dog could make in an otherwise grim situation.

"Thank you for sharing your dog with us," Mariella said. "It means a lot that you all have come. Everything is so frightening right now. At this point we don't even know if we have a house to go home to. Tugger and his smiles and hugs really brightened the girls' day, and ours, as well."

"We're just happy we can be here to help in any way we can," Stone said, handing Jason eight bottles of water from the wagon he was pulling. The smile suddenly dropped from Stone's face. "This can't be easy. We'll be praying for you."

Jason pinched his lips and shook his

head, unable to respond, and Felicity's heart clenched for the poor family.

As they said their goodbyes to Ariana and Lily and moved onward, Stone took Felicity by the elbow. "There is so much need here," he whispered. "I can't even imagine how it would feel to be in Jason's position, possibly losing his house and being helpless to do anything about it."

"You're right," Felicity agreed. "But praise God their whole family made it out alive and safe." She sighed deeply. "This isn't my first disaster relief response call, but it never gets easier, seeing all these people suffering. That's why what we do—and what our dogs do—is so important. Reaching out and lifting people's spirits when they've been brought low really is a ministry."

He nodded slowly. "I just watched how God used you to bring joy to that family. But I want to help, too—the way you and Tugger do. Show me how to work with Dandy."

She had to admit she was surprised at how earnest Stone's expression and voice were. As much as she'd crushed over him in her youth, she'd also known him to be self-centered and egotistical. But she supposed everyone had to grow up sometime. People changed and matured.

Even Stone Keller.

Felicity's attention was quickly diverted when a group of noisy, chattering little girls approached, all wanting to be the first to pet Tugger. She crouched next to the dog and allowed them to coo and fawn over him, knowing Tugger was enjoying every minute and wouldn't be put off by the noise. Little girls were his specialty.

It was several minutes before she glanced up and noticed Stone standing nearby, looking as lost as a stray kitten. His arms were crossed over his muscular chest and he was shifting from boot to boot as if he couldn't stand still but didn't know where to go. Dandy was by his side, looking up at the man as if the Lab didn't quite know what to do with him. He was waiting for direction from Stone and finding none, which made Dandy appear antsy, as well.

It was time to give him some guidance. There were so many people in this gym who needed what Stone and Dandy could offer.

Felicity glanced around, noticing a dark-haired little boy in the far corner of the gym who looked a bit older than most of the children. Middle school, she guessed. He was sitting alone in the center of his cot with his feet up and a blanket covering his shoulders, curled into himself and appearing downright miserable. But what Felicity really noticed was the way his eyes were glued on Dandy.

No—not Dandy.

While nearly all the children were taken in by the dogs, this boy was looking straight at Stone, pushing his dark hair out of his eyes when it flopped over his forehead. If she wasn't mistaken, there was a glint of recognition, perhaps even admiration, in his gaze.

Was it possible this boy somehow knew Stone?

Chapter Three

Stone heard his name and turned his attention to Felicity, who was coming his way with Tugger and a gaggle of girls at her heels. It looked as if she'd picked up a flock of happy little birds, cheeping and chirping and not acting at all like they were in the middle of difficult circumstances.

Finally. He was beginning to think she'd completely abandoned him. He had no idea what to do without her, and felt foolish just waiting for her, doing nothing. He'd spent the majority of his life choosing the wrong things, and now that he was faced with the opportunity to do something positive, he was stymied. He'd always been outgoing, often exasperatingly so, but now anyone looking at him would think he was an introvert, standing around watching, without doing anything to help. He wanted to be like Felicity, making the rounds with her dog in tow, but he was so afraid he'd do the wrong thing that he'd ended up doing nothing.

"I think you have an admirer."

Heat rose to his face. "What?"

"Shh. Don't be too obvious about it," Felicity said with a soft smile, leaning in close enough to his ear that he could feel the warmth of her breath, "but take a look at the dark-haired boy sitting over there in the corner. Any chance you know him?"

Stone flushed in relief that the admirer she was referring to wasn't some previous lady friend of his. He was working hard on his reputation and had hoped it wouldn't follow him home. Leaning back and swiveling on his heels, he glanced at the boy in question and then back at Felicity, shaking his head in bemusement. "No. I don't think so. Why?"

"Maybe I'm mistaken, but he's been watching you like a hawk since you first arrived. He can't take his eyes off you, and I have the oddest sensation that he knows you."

He lifted his cowboy hat and shoved his hand back through his hair. "Hmm. I don't see how. I don't recognize him, but let me go talk to him."

This was giving him some sense of direction, anyway, even if he wasn't nearly as good at interacting with children as Felicity was. The truth was, he was feeling a little nervous about it. Still, this young man was definitely a place to start.

"Come along?" he asked Felicity hopefully. It wouldn't be nearly as difficult with her by his side.

Her grin widened and she nodded, then explained to the little girls crowded around her dog that other people in the gym also needed to pet Tugger to feel better. Somehow, she managed to extricate herself from the group by suggesting that the girls play a game of tag in the hallway, which they immediately picked up on, running off with their laughter trailing behind them.

Stone felt surprisingly cool and collected as he approached the young, wide-eyed boy. He thought perhaps God was offering an extra sense of peace to calm his nerves. He'd been so uneasy coming into this disaster relief situation, and he'd felt as useless as a statue in the middle of the road while waiting for Felicity until a few minutes ago. Unloading truckloads of supplies hadn't been too bad, since he'd used his muscles rather than his brains, but now he was seeing what Felicity saw, and the reason she'd rushed to the scene despite her own issues. They might not be able to fix the situation. Many people were really and truly displaced, and this was only the first of many challenging days. But Felicity understood the real need here today was to reach out to the people's hearts, to bring some happiness and joy in the form of the service dogs.

Granted, not everyone wanted to interact with the dogs, much less the adult humans accompanying them, but for maybe the first time in his life, Stone felt as if he had the opportunity to make a real difference in someone's life. And that was saying something, coming from a cowboy who'd spent most of his life thinking only of himself.

"Hello, there," he said to the little boy. "Is it okay if I sit here?" He pointed to a folding chair that had been set up near the child.

The boy just pinched his lips together and shrugged as if he didn't care one way or the other. He didn't quite make eye contact with Stone but instead stared intently at his lap.

Felicity held back and watched, allowing Stone to take the lead without her interference—although Stone half wished she'd step in and help.

"Thanks," Stone said, sitting down and nonchalantly moving Dandy between him and the boy, hoping the dog would know what to do without too many commands on his part. He hadn't heard Felicity saying much to direct Tugger with the girls, yet Tugger was a natural with all the kids. So far, Stone hadn't really seen Dandy do much other than pull a toboggan, but hopefully, Dandy would have the same skills as Tugger.

As if on cue, Dandy put his nose on the boy's knee and snuffled closer, but the youngster didn't immediately respond. He stayed curled inside his blanket, quietly rocking back and forth.

Self-soothing, Stone guessed. He couldn't even begin to imagine what the poor child had been through today.

"My name's Stone," he said, not really expecting to make a two-way conversation but opening it up in case the boy wanted to share his name.

"I know," the boy replied, almost casually.

Stone stared at him in confusion for a moment before replying.

"You do?"

"Yep. Sure do."

Stone waited for an explanation but apparently none was forthcoming. He met Felicity's eyes and widened his gaze in a silent plea for her to rescue him. He was way out of his depth here and his brain was tripping all over itself trying to find the right response.

Felicity approached and knelt in front of the boy. "Hi. I'm Felicity and this is Dandy. Do you like dogs?"

He jerked his chin in a short nod and then brushed his palm across Dandy's head.

Felicity gestured to the Lab and then the pit bull. "Our other dog is named Tugger. What's your name?"

The boy hesitated and then finally answered, "Myles," as if the word was being pulled from him like a painful tooth.

"Myles here told me he knew my name was Stone even before I introduced myself," Stone offered, not certain how to get to the bottom of this mystery. Felicity had probably heard what the boy had said, but Stone thought maybe if he highlighted the interaction Myles might explain further.

"Yeah," Myles agreed, scoffing under his breath and rolling his eyes as if it were obvious. "That's cuz I do."

Myles clearly didn't want anyone to know this introduction mattered to him, but somehow Stone could feel that it did. If only he could work out how and why.

"And you know Stone from...?" Felicity asked, letting the sentence dangle for the boy to finish.

"Duh. He's famous. Everybody knows him."

Since it was a small town, most people in Whispering Pines knew him from the time he was knee-high to a grasshopper, but Holden Springs was some distance away from Whispering Pines and it wasn't likely that everybody knew him there.

But people who followed rodeo would know him.

"Rodeo," Stone guessed aloud, relief sounding in his voice. Suddenly it all made sense.

"Of course," Felicity agreed. "Stone is a

famous rodeo rider. Do you like watching rodeo, Myles?"

Myles nodded so fervently that a lock of dark hair fell down over his forehead. He pushed it up with his palm before explaining.

"Stone is my very favorite bareback rider of all time. I've saved all the programs from whenever my mom took me to a rodeo where he was riding, and I also get a monthly magazine that used to have Stone in it all the time. Only now he's never in there anymore because he got in that motorcycle accident and so he doesn't ride."

He gave Stone the stink-eye and Stone nearly cracked up, though he was careful to stay composed. Clearly it meant a lot to Myles that his favorite cowboy was no longer riding in the ring.

"I appreciate that you've followed my career," Stone said. "And I'm really sorry about the accident."

He couldn't help that his ego swelled a bit. The little boy really did know all about him. He'd dealt with tons of fans over the years, but none felt as important as the one who was now sitting in front of him. His mind scrambled for an idea as to how to make this visit special for Myles, especially given the poor kid's current circumstances.

Having obviously overheard the conversation, a young woman, whom Stone guessed to be the boy's mother, came to Stone's rescue.

"Myles here is quite the artist," the woman, who introduced herself as Anna, complimented. She tenderly brushed the boy's hair back off his forehead, where once again a lock had fallen into eyes that were as dark as his hair. "He loves to draw and paint and make sculptures out of clay."

"Yeah?" asked Stone. "That's pretty awesome. What kinds of stuff do you draw?"

"Horses, mostly," Myles admitted softly, still not making eye contact with Stone but reaching out to pet Dandy's head. The dog immediately responded by drawing nearer and resting his muzzle on the boy's knee.

Was it Stone's imagination or were Myles's shoulders a little less tense now? Stone was amazed at how therapeutic the dogs really were. He'd had no idea until today, and he probably wouldn't have believed it without seeing it for himself. Dandy reached Myles in a way no human could.

Stone had an idea he wanted to try, but he was aware just how fast this interaction could go south if he was wrong, knowing the boy's family might have had to evacuate quickly. He debated for a moment before asking, "Do you have any of your drawings here that I could see? Or could you maybe draw me a new one?"

Myles stared at him for a long moment before turning to his mother and nodding. "Guess so. I think my mama has them."

Anna, who had also been petting Dandy, grabbed a dinosaur backpack nearby and dug around for a moment before pulling out a folder brimming with amazingly lifelike drawings of horses from all angles, some full body, and others only heads. The boy had definitely studied equine anatomy, because every one of these pictures was spot-on. And Stone could tell how much Myles loved the rodeo, by the poses in which the horses had been drawn. Not only standing, walking and galloping, but roping and bucking. They were so specific and true to life Stone was fairly certain he recognized some of the horses as actual ones he'd ridden in the circuit.

"Hey—is that horse Barn Burner?" he

asked, holding his breath as he awaited an answer from the boy. He wouldn't have dared ask except the drawing appeared to be the exact replica of the beast who had thrown Stone on numerous occasions. He totally knew that horse more than any of the others he'd ridden over the years—and way better than he wanted to. He had suffered far too many bumps and bruises to prove their encounters. It was only on the last ride that Stone had finally reached the coveted eight seconds on Barn Burner.

Myles nodded, and Stone thought he caught the wisp of a smile cross the boy's otherwise serious expression.

"I am completely amazed by your talent," Felicity praised, her smile encouraging Myles. "These horses are beautiful."

"I'm also impressed," Stone added. "You know that Barn Burner threw me a few times before my last ride, but I finally got the best of him. I barely made those eight seconds, but man, was that a rush!"

He wasn't bragging. He was just trying to connect the picture to a story and hopefully induce another smile out of Myles.

"I know," was all Myles said, and Stone's heart welled as he chuckled.

"Did you see me that evening?" he asked. "When I finally bested that wretched horse?"

He finally got the smile he'd been hoping for when Myles said, "I was in the front row, cheering for you."

Stone held up his hand and Myles gave him an enthusiastic high five.

Stone didn't know what Myles's story was, whether he and his mom had lost their house to the avalanche or were just temporarily displaced, but either way, Stone was definitely going to be praying for him and his mother.

"Why don't you autograph the picture of Barn Burner for Myles?" Felicity suggested, excitement lining her tone at the novel idea.

"Well, I don't know." Stone hesitated, not wanting to be too forward. Of course he'd been asked for his autograph before, but what if the boy didn't want him scribbling all over his masterpiece?

"What do you think, Myles? Would you like Stone's autograph on Barn Burner?" Anna asked.

"Wow. I sure would!" Myles suddenly came alive as he handed the drawing to

Stone. Finally, Stone felt as if they'd truly connected.

Anna unzipped the front pocket of the backpack and retrieved a drawing pencil, handing it to Stone for him to scribble his name on the bottom corner of the picture.

To Myles:
Stay Strong!
Stone Keller.

He handed the pencil and the drawing back to Myles, who put it in his lap and stared down at it with a slight smile hovering on his lips. "This is awesome. My friends are never gonna believe it!"

"Myles is in the junior rodeo league at his school," Anna explained. "He's learning to ride bareback."

"Just like you," Myles added enthusiastically, and somehow Stone knew the boy would remember this day as something special no matter what other circumstances had happened to him. Likewise, Anna couldn't thank him enough.

Yet, unlike so many years in his past, Stone didn't need the attention or the gratitude to stroke his ego. It was enough that he'd connected with this little boy and had made his otherwise awful day better.

It had made Stone's day better, as well. This was certainly a day he would never forget, not the disaster and certainly not the people he'd met, and he offered silent thanks to God that Felicity had allowed him to come along.

Felicity and Stone spent another two hours in the gym, passing out water to displaced families and allowing children and adults alike to play and interact with the dogs. Other volunteers were preparing a hot meal in the high school cafeteria to make sure everyone was fed. Stone had never seen so many people cheerfully willing to lend a helping hand, and his head and heart were so full he thought he might burst.

In one afternoon, he'd truly learned about what it meant to reach out in love to others, and what he'd experienced here would not soon leave him.

"So, what did you think?" Felicity asked him when they were back on the highway on their way to Whispering Pines. "Do you believe it was worth your while?"

"I'll say. I don't know what I'd imagined it

would be like to volunteer for disaster relief, but that was not it. The way the kids especially interacted with the dogs is something I'll never forget."

"I know, right? Those people—they're all dealing with unimaginable circumstances. Anything we can do to help seems like too little."

"That boy—Myles. I was shocked at first when he said he knew who I was. I couldn't figure it out at all."

"I can't imagine you've suddenly started underestimating yourself," she teased. "Or your fan base."

He chuckled. "I deserve that, though I'd like to think I've matured since the last time I was in Whispering Pines."

"Time will tell."

He'd gotten her eyes sparkling, at least for a second, and it was all he could do not to blurt out how much she'd matured and how much he admired her after what he'd seen today, working with the dogs and the displaced people.

But he knew better than that, and reminded himself to keep a sock in it. Felicity was as off-limits as a woman could be. She had flashing stop signs all around her. And Sharpe would probably knock his lights out just hearing their banter, much less discovering Felicity had caught Stone's eye even for the slightest moment.

He took a huge mental step backward.

"It was amazing working with the dogs, especially with the kids. How did you train them to be so open and not freak out when kids suddenly run over and hug them?"

"Mostly, it's just a matter of socialization. Not every dog has the right temperament, but when they do, it's more about focusing on whether or not a specific child has an interest in whatever dog I've got with me than how the dog will react. Or focusing on the *man* I've got with me, in the case of you and Myles. You could just tell he was so thrilled to meet you in person, even before you got him to open up."

"It was different than any other fan interaction I've ever had," Stone said, happy to be back on the subject of the little boy who'd so touched his heart. "Myles didn't quite make eye contact with me most of the time. He totally blew me away when I introduced myself and he said he already knew my name. You saw how flustered I got. It's a good thing you were there to dig me out."

"Always a pleasure." She tossed a saucy grin at him. "I work search and rescue. Digging is a special skill of mine."

"There'll be a time when it will be my turn to come to your rescue," he assured her. "And when that time comes, you can count on me."

He knew in that moment they were just flirting, but he was perfectly serious about what he'd just told her.

He would be there for her, and that was one promise he intended to keep.

Felicity was feeling all talked out as Stone drove them back to Whispering Pines. If he felt inclined to speak, he didn't say so, though his expression was thoughtful, and he glanced at her often. Though she stared out the passenger window at the winding road and snow-covered scenery, she instinctively felt whenever his gaze was on her.

After a good fifteen minutes of driving without saying a word to spoil the silence, Stone finally cleared his throat.

"I'm going to take you to urgent care." It

was a statement, not a question, and his voice popped Felicity right out of her reverie.

"What?" she asked, snapping her head around to meet his eyes.

"There's no use trying to hide it from me, Felicity. I can see your pain clearly written on your face. You overdid it big-time today. You spent the whole day on your feet with nothing more than the bandage we wrapped earlier. You need to have your ankle looked at, and that's the end of the subject."

The command in his voice might have felt overbearing if it weren't for the sheer compassion in his gaze. She could tell he was worried about her, and it warmed her heart. Still, she didn't want him to be concerned when he needn't be.

She tried to shrug him off, but it turned out looking more like a wince. Now that she thought about it, her ankle was kind of throbbing from her being on her feet all day, but it hadn't really bothered her until this moment, and that wasn't really why she was hurting.

"It's my heart, not my ankle," she admitted, her voice cracking with emotion. "Definitely not anything Urgent Care can cure."

Stone found a safe spot on the road to pull

over. He put the truck in Park and turned to face her.

"What do you mean?" he asked gently. "Talk to me."

"It's always difficult to see people in these temporary disaster shelters, knowing how much they may have lost and how their lives changed so significantly in a single day, sometimes even less than that." She sighed. "It just breaks my heart all over the place. I spent many hours this past summer out visiting people displaced by wildfires in shelters similar to the shelter we visited today. The dogs really made a difference there, too."

"But?" he asked, evidently sensing she wasn't sharing the whole story.

"It's the avalanche."

"There have been far too many avalanches this year—way more than last year," he agreed. "It seems like it's getting worse and worse."

"Yes. Avalanches are the worst. And I lost someone…important to me," she admitted, her voice a ragged whisper. "Last year. In a freak accident."

He reached out and clasped her hand in his. "I'm so sorry. That must be awful for you, especially seeing how much people's lives have changed because of the avalanche today."

She shook her head and sniffed. "His name was Trevor. Honestly, I don't talk about it much, not even to my brothers and sisters."

His brow lowered. "You don't have to talk about it now to me if you don't want to, but I'd like to think I'm a good listener."

She chuckled through her tears. "I'm afraid if I don't tell you what's really on my heart, you're going to hustle me off to the hospital to get a cast on my ankle whether I like it or not."

Somehow finding humor in the situation lightened her mood, especially when Stone answered with a smile of his own.

"Guilty as charged. Someone has to take care of you," he teased.

His empathetic response gave her the courage to continue. Her siblings had all been there to help her through the darkest part of her life, but even though she still suffered many periods of grief and was grasping to keep her faith alive, she didn't speak of Trevor's accident much now. She didn't want to be a burden to anyone.

She couldn't even believe she was sitting

here alone talking with, of all people, her teenage crush, and sharing with him major life problems. In a million years, who would have ever thought this could happen? They'd both certainly come a long way since her middle school days.

Still, here was Stone with a welcome and open attitude, not pressuring her in any way to share more than she was able but offering a willing ear if she was so inclined to speak.

"Trevor was my ex-boyfriend. We'd had quite a serious relationship—or at least, I thought so at the time. We'd been discussing getting married and starting a family before we split up."

"What happened?" Stone's blue eyes darkened and his grip on her hand tightened.

"I don't really know. Trevor was a kid at heart and a serious risk-taker. Always chasing a new thrill. I should have known he wasn't ready to settle down and get married, much less start a family. All he wanted to do was find new ways to play."

Stone tightly pressed his lips together into a hard, straight line, and Felicity realized she could have been talking about Stone himself, the ultimate bad boy and risk-taker. As a rodeo cowboy, he'd never settled in one place for too long. Even the motorcycle accident that ruined his rodeo career had been from reckless driving.

"Trevor balked when I finally pressed him for a commitment," Felicity continued, dropping Stone's hand to wrap her arms around herself. "Maybe that wasn't fair to him. I knew he wasn't ready to change his lifestyle. But we'd been together for two years and for my part I was ready to take the next steps, to plan out our future together."

"That's reasonable," Stone assured her. "Two years is a long time to date."

"At the time, I thought so, too." The corner of her lips twitched. "Trevor, not so much. He resisted change of any kind, and I should have known better than to try to make him into someone he wasn't. We got into a huge fight, he left screeching out of the driveway in his truck, and that was the last time I ever saw him alive."

"What happened?"

"Trevor and his friends went snowboarding off-grid in the Rocky Mountains. They weren't supposed to be where they were. But black diamond slopes weren't enough for Trevor. He had to go find his own mountain to conquer."

She closed her eyes and took a deep breath before uttering her next words. "They caused a major avalanche. His friends got out of it alive. Trevor didn't."

"Wow," Stone said with a low whistle. "I'm truly sorry. That's a large burden for you to carry, though I hope you know it's not your fault Trevor wasn't ready to change." He cleared his throat, but his voice was still as deep and raspy as it always was. "Men can change. Or rather, I've learned God can change our hearts."

"Maybe. I just feel as if that part of my life is so unresolved. Like, how could God have let that accident happen after we'd argued? I mean, there's no good time for someone young to die like that, but it was just too much for me. I went through a really dark time in my life for many months after Trevor's death, and I'm still struggling to understand why God did what He did. Then, seeing these people today…"

"I can totally understand how avalanches would trigger you. Frankly, I'm surprised you even agreed to go today. That can't have been easy for you."

"It wasn't. I crammed down my fears because people there needed help, and I can't ignore the needs of others no matter how I feel in my own heart. Today wasn't about me. I did what I had to do."

"Wow," he said over a breath, and then tipped his hat at her. "That takes guts. No wonder you're gritting your teeth now."

She only shrugged and turned back to the window, though she consciously concentrated on loosening her jaw as Stone put the truck in gear and turned back onto the road.

Guts she had in abundance. She had a heart because she felt the pain of heartache on a daily basis.

No—what was missing from her life was spirit. It would take the Spirit of God to bring her back to anything resembling a real life, and she didn't see that happening anytime soon.

As she'd told Stone, she did what she had to do. But it was no longer a ministry, bringing therapy dogs into disaster situations and reaching out to the people there.

She was no longer serving God, only her fellow man.

She wished that was enough.

But she knew it wasn't.

Chapter Four

"How are you feeling, Mama?" Stone asked as his mother shuffled into the kitchen in jeans, a too-loose blue sweater that used to fit her and slip-on shoes, hiding a yawn beneath her palm. He was amazed by how cheerful she was despite the weekly chemotherapy, which had at times brought her so physically low. She'd shaved her head before her hair had started falling out, saying she wasn't going to let cancer have the privilege of taking that away from her. Rather, she had made it be her own choice.

She was a fighter, and that was how she faced every hurdle in her life, including stage three metastatic breast cancer. She'd had surgery when Stone was still recuperating in the hospital from his accident, and was now nearing the end of chemo.

He'd hated that he couldn't be by her side then, but he was now, and he was determined to stay here until she'd beaten this thing. She had good days and bad days, though Stone was worried that the bad days were becoming much more prevalent. She silently suffered through agonizing side effects. And she'd lost a considerable amount of weight in the four months since she'd been diagnosed.

As he'd told Felicity, taking care of his mother was the primary reason for his return to Whispering Pines after getting out of the hospital following his motorcycle accident. Otherwise he might not have come back at all. He had a job waiting for him at a rodeo school in Wyoming, but it would still be there after his mother felt better.

And he prayed with all his heart and without ceasing that she would get better, go into remission and beat cancer. If anyone could, it was Mama.

"I made your favorite," Stone said, turning away from the stove and pulling out a chair for his mother.

"My gallant son," she said, sighing with relief as she slid into the chair. Then her gaze narrowed on him. "But as far as my favorite breakfast is concerned, eggs, bacon, toast and broiled tomatoes doesn't even sound appetizing right now."

He chuckled. "Okay, so maybe I didn't make your very favorite." He spooned oatmeal into two bowls. "But I have fresh cream and brown sugar to add to the cereal, and it's easy on the mouth."

He placed the bowls on the table and slid into the seat beside her. After he prayed a blessing over the food, she reached out her hand and pressed her palm to his scruffy cheek. "I don't know what I did to deserve a son like you."

"Oh, Mama." He was suddenly choked up, and didn't know if he could swallow a spoonful of oatmeal if he tried.

The truth was, Stone didn't deserve her, a single mother who'd struggled to make ends meet and put food on the table his whole life, who'd scrimped and saved and spent nothing on herself in order to make a college fund he hadn't even ended up using. She'd put her whole life into Stone even during those stressful years when he'd made things difficult for her. It shamed him that there had been a time in his life when he hadn't even given her health and wellbeing a second thought.

He'd been a selfish brat as a teenager and young adult. He could only hope he could make it up to her now that he was back. He was certainly going to try to do his best.

"I have a surprise for you today," he told her. Stone noticed his mother was moving her spoon around in the bowl without actually scooping any into her mouth, though he didn't let her know he was observing her with concern.

Her eyes lit up. "Will you tell me, or do I have to guess?"

He grinned. "I know you love surprises, Mama, but you'd never guess what I've got planned for you. I'm bringing a guest with us to the hospital today to keep you entertained." The chemo infusions often took three or four hours or more. Sometimes Stone read to her. Other times, they played cards or a board game. Often, she was simply too worn out by the treatment to do anything and dozed while Stone caught up on his email or social media on his cell phone.

"Word has it she is a great gin rummy player. I know that's your favorite game."

"She?" his mother said, perking up, her eyes brightening. "Is this a special she you're talking about?"

Heat rose to Stone's face. "Simmer down, Mama," he said with a laugh, holding up his hands in surrender. "Much as I know you'd love it, this isn't a date."

She scoffed. "Well, I have to say I'm actually happy to hear that. Taking your mama to a chemo session would be the worst date ever recorded in the history of mankind. I hope I've raised a son with better sense than that."

He snorted.

"You're much better company that I'd ever be for a young lady," Mama teased. "With or without the chemo."

"Who said anything about her being young?" he asked, starting to feel genuinely flustered by his mother's teasing.

She raised her penciled-in eyebrows. Her own had fallen out from the chemo.

"Yeah, okay," he reluctantly admitted. "She's young."

"And pretty?"

"That, too. But Mama, we're just developing a friendship here. Barely that, since I've just come back to town. And even if I were interested in her that way, which I'm not, friendship is all it can ever be."

"I see," Mama said.

Oh, she so didn't see, although Stone wasn't sure how much he wanted to admit. Talk about an awkward conversation to be having with his mama, of all people.

He was beginning to think inviting Felicity along today had been a bad idea, but she'd actually been the one to suggest it after he mentioned he'd need an afternoon off from working at Winslow's Woodlands to accompany his mother to her chemo treatment. As he was quickly learning about Felicity, she always wanted to step up and help other people.

And she was as stubborn as she was heartfelt.

He desperately wanted to shift this conversation with his mom into reverse and steer it in another direction, but he knew he wasn't going to get out of this unscathed, so he finally admitted, "It's Felicity Winslow. Sharpe's little sister. I've been working with her ever since I got back into town."

"Ahhh," Mama said in a long-drawn-out breath followed by a wide smile. "Now I really do understand. Felicity is all grown up now and has turned into a very pretty young lady, but dating your best friend's little sister is not quite the thing, is it? Doesn't it go against the Man Code or something?"

Stone threw back his head and laughed. "Oh, Mama. *Man Code?* Really? But you're right. Sharpe would tan my hide if I so much as asked Felicity out on a date," he admitted with a grin. "And as far as Felicity being the little sister—she may be younger than Sharpe and me, but she's all grown up now." His face heated even as he said the words.

His mother clapped her hands together, a big grin on her face.

"Seriously, Mama? You can tease me all you want, but please, *please* don't put Felicity on the spot. She's still not over Trevor, and I wouldn't want to do anything to accidentally upset her."

He didn't feel the need to elaborate. Whispering Pines was a small town. Mama probably knew more about Felicity and Trevor than he did.

"Of course not, darling," Mama said, patting his hand. "You're the only one in my life I love to tease."

Just then, the doorbell rang, relieving Stone from having to continue this awkward conversation. He took a deep breath and let it out slowly, trying to pull himself together.

He opened the door to find a fresh-faced, smiling Felicity, her blond hair pulled back into a ponytail as usual and threaded through the back of her ball cap, rocking her blue jeans and a white Aran sweater.

He shouldn't be noticing these things. Sharpe would have something to say about Stone's thoughts, were he to find out about them.

Which he wouldn't.

Stone blinked and swallowed hard, determined to shelve these errant feelings into the back of his mind somewhere.

But it was going to be harder than he thought.

Felicity had opted not to put on her usual light pink blush today. For one thing, it was a crisp winter's day, and the wind was blowing bits of snow in the air, and for another, just being around Stone brought a consistent blush to her cheeks even without the blush.

As much as she was trying not to think about him, she couldn't seem to help the way her mind kept drifting back to her teenage years. The thought embarrassed her now, but she supposed she hadn't acted any differently than any other lovestruck teenager, hoping that someday Stone would suddenly notice her out of nowhere and declare his undying love for her.

Of course, back then, Stone was a senior in high school and only into himself and his precious rodeo. He would no more have noticed Sharpe's angst-ridden little sister than the ground under his feet. Girls his own age flocked to him like birds on a tree, but he never favored any one in particular.

Forcing her thoughts back to the present, she glanced at her cell phone and then back up at Stone.

"Sorry. I'm a little early," she apologized, and the expected heat rushed to her cheeks the moment her gaze met Stone's. There was the blush.

"Early is good. Mama and I were just finishing up our breakfast. Come on in and I'll pour you a cup of coffee."

She followed Stone into the kitchen, where Colleen Keller was sitting with a mostly uneaten bowl of oatmeal in front of her, sipping a cup of green tea.

"Don't get up," Felicity said, hurrying around the table to give Colleen a gentle hug and a kiss on her cheek. It didn't escape her notice that the poor woman's shoulder bones were protruding out from under her sweater.

"No sense lollygagging about just because chemo infusions are no fun," Colleen said, standing with Felicity's support. "Stone, pour those cups of coffee for you and Felicity into travel mugs and let's get this over with."

Felicity and Colleen kept up friendly chatter on the way to the hospital. Felicity was doing all she could to keep Colleen's spirits up. She didn't know exactly what went into a chemo treatment, but she knew it couldn't possibly be comfortable and that it came with many side effects. The less Colleen had to dwell on it, the better.

Stone remained silent as he drove his mother's silver SUV into Lakewood, where the hospital with the best cancer treatment center was. It was a long drive, over an hour, and Felicity imagined that time in the vehicle only added to Colleen's discomfort, though the older woman didn't say anything about it. Stone had tucked pillows around Colleen before they'd left the house, and Felicity now knew why. She noticed Stone wasn't contributing much to the conversation, despite her repeated attempts to include him.

She wondered if maybe he was regretting allowing her to come, if perhaps he thought she was sticking her nose in family business. After all, she had rather invited herself, and she was now carrying the majority of the conversation.

But Colleen had been good friends with Felicity's mother before she had passed away, and Felicity somehow sensed her mother would have appreciated her reaching out to the Kellers in their time of need.

If she could do anything to make Colleen's burden any lighter, she would. She only hoped Stone wouldn't cop an attitude that would ruin everyone's day. He hadn't really given her any reason to think he would. He'd been a different man since returning to Whispering Pines. But today he was being awfully quiet—too quiet, and Felicity couldn't help but wonder why.

He appeared to pull himself together when they reached the hospital. He doted on his mother, first opening the back passenger door for Felicity and then the front for Colleen, lending both arms to steady her as she exited the vehicle and then keeping a strong arm around her waist and a hand on her elbow.

His genuine care for his mother was obvious both on his face and in his actions, and Felicity's heart caught in her throat. She felt bad that she'd doubted him even for a moment.

"I brought playing cards to pass the time," Colleen said as a nurse hooked an IV to her chest port for her infusion. She leaned back in her plush armchair and sighed tiredly as Stone tucked the blue-and-orange crochet blanket around her that he'd brought with him.

"We don't have to play cards," Felicity assured her, pulling up a chair and reaching for Colleen's hand, covering it with her other hand when she realized how cold Colleen's fingers were. "I'm fine just sitting here keeping you company."

Stone pulled up another chair on his mother's other side. "You can even doze if you want," he suggested. "You look tired, Mama."

"I don't want to pass up the opportunity for you to beat me at gin rummy," she teased Felicity with a weary laugh.

Stone shuffled the cards, but his mother was quietly dozing before he had so much as dealt the first hand.

"Poor Mama," Stone whispered, his voice coarse with emotion, his shiny-eyed gaze meeting Felicity's. "She tries so hard not to show all the struggles she's facing, but I've heard her sobbing in pain in the middle of the night when she thinks I can't hear."

"I'm so sorry. I had no idea it was this bad."

He shook his head and scoffed. "Neither did I until I moved back home. It's not as if she'd talk about it, not even when we were on video chats together back when I was in the hospital. She's a proud woman. But there are days now when she can't even get out of bed. And there's nothing—" he punched a fist into his open palm "—*nothing* I can do for her, other than give her a pain pill and hope it will be enough to allow her to get some rest."

Felicity was feeling equally helpless at the moment, unable to assist Colleen or Stone. She reached for his closed fist and massaged it out until his hand was no longer clenched.

"You're here with her now, supporting her through this rough time in her life. That's a lot, Stone. I'd venture to guess that for your mother, your presence here in her life now is the very best thing you can give her."

"I hate cancer," he spat out vehemently and dropped his gaze from hers. "I wasn't a good son to her, you know. Before. I never thought about her at all when I was out making the rodeo rounds. I have a lot to make up for. I hope God gives me that time."

"Maybe you do need to make things right with her," she agreed, not to rub salt in the wound so much as to get to the real point. "But right now the fact that you're here with her, in her life and by her side, gives her strength and comfort she can't find any-where else."

He picked off his hat and scrubbed a hand through his reddish gold hair. "Yeah, maybe.

But I hate not being able to do anything useful to help her through her trials. It's such a helpless feeling. I don't like it."

"But you *are* being useful, in more ways than just taking up room in your house. She told me on the drive down that you cooked her breakfast this morning."

Stone clicked his tongue. "Oatmeal. Big deal."

"Still. That's one thing she doesn't have to do for herself. And you help her manage her cocktail of pills every day and bring her extra pillows when she needs them. You make sure she has the TV remote and any books at her bedside she'd like to read."

He scoffed and shook his head. "That's the least I can do."

"Yes," Felicity agreed, a cacophony of emotions singing through her. "And the most."

Their eyes met and held, his gaze a mixture of anger and surprising vulnerability.

The next moment, his eyes became hooded and he swallowed hard before turning away.

Chapter Five

Stone was nervous.

Which was ridiculous. He had absolutely nothing to be nervous about. He was taking Preacher and Deacon, Winslow's Woodlands' matched gray Percheron horses, out on a practice sleigh ride before he started driving daily visitors out on the sleigh in earnest. As a teenager, he'd often pitched in, driving the sleigh for farm guests while Sharpe and Frost were busy during their Christmas and Winterfest seasons, and he'd also driven the cart for the hayrack rides come spring and summer.

He knew all three routes by heart and what to expect with each one. He knew the horses well, as they'd been there back when Stone was in high school. And he was a horse guy, after all—a cowboy through and through who'd been riding as long as he'd been walking. He could communicate with horses at least as well as with humans.

No. It wasn't the horses or the job or the fact that he hadn't driven a sleigh in years, he realized as he led the first draft, Preacher, to the front of the sleigh and harnessed him up.

If he was being honest with himself, these deep-seated, gut-flipping feelings had to do with Felicity, who'd be accompanying him on the ride today, ostensibly to make sure he didn't run into any issues his first time out on the route.

He was perfectly aware she knew she didn't need to come along. There was nothing Stone could run into that he wouldn't be able to handle on his own. Her motives were suspect, which made him wonder why she was really accompanying him.

He couldn't say he actually minded, whatever her intentions. The more time he spent with Felicity, the more he liked her—which he kept entirely to himself. If Sharpe had the slightest inkling Stone and Felicity were becoming good friends, Stone would probably be ousted from his job without a reference.

Sharpe had always been protective of all four of his sisters, and that was especially true of the "baby" in the family, Felicity.

Felicity showed up at the barn with Tugger and Dandy at her heels just as he finished hooking the second Percheron, Deke, to the sleigh and making sure both horses were comfortable and ready to pull.

"I can't wait for the ride," she said, clapping her mittened hands together. Dandy ran around Stone's feet and barked with equal enthusiasm. "This is such a rare treat for me, and I've really been looking forward to it. I'm usually too busy working in the gift shop to take a sleigh ride just for fun. It was nice of Ruby to cover for me so I could come with you today."

He chuckled at her eagerness. She was bundled up for the weather in black snow boots tied with little white pom-poms, a bright pink puffer jacket, a thick white crochet scarf tightly wrapped around her neck, a pale pink stocking cap with another white pom-pom on top and thick white crocheted mittens. Her cheeks were already as pink as her coat from the crisp winter air and her breath was coming out in shallow puffs.

As if she was reading his thoughts, she looked him over from head to toe. "Aren't you going to freeze to death on the ride? The temperature isn't going to rise above freezing today and the wind is blowing something fierce." She shivered for emphasis.

He glanced down at his long-sleeved Western shirt, black puffer vest, jeans with his leather work gloves tucked into the left back pocket and the hiking boots he'd exchanged from his usual cowboy boots, which were too slick for him to wear in the snow. As always, he wore his cowboy hat, the one item of clothing that never changed.

"I can run back up to the house and grab you a knit hat and a scarf, at least," she offered, but he shook his head.

"I'm plenty warm, thanks. I'll be fine with what I've got on." His metabolism had always run as warm as a woodstove, now more than ever since he'd bulked up his physique. His muscles kept him plenty warm. He wasn't even sure he really needed his vest, but after Felicity's remarks he decided to keep it on.

"Suit yourself. But I'm going to tell you I told you so when you're turning into an ice cube. It gets mighty cold up there on the sleigh with the wind and the snow blowing in your face. You've probably forgotten freezing to death as you drive."

"No, I remember how cold it gets. Is that why you're so bundled up you can barely move and all I can see is your eyes peeking out?" he teased.

"Better safe than sorry. I'm almost always cold. I wear a sweater in the summer when the air conditioning comes on."

"Weird," he said, keeping his expression totally neutral. "But then, the more time we're spending together, the more I'm really discovering that about you."

She huffed and swatted his shoulder.

He laughed before gesturing to the sleigh. "Here. Let me give you a lift up."

"I don't—" she started, but by this time he'd grasped her waist, picked her up and plunked her into the seat before she could even so much as finish her sentence.

"Oh," she exclaimed. "Thanks." He suspected she'd been about to tell him she'd been crawling up on the sleigh by herself since she was a little girl, but it was too late for that now. She called to the dogs, who jumped into the back seat of the sleigh on their own, barking wildly in their excitement.

"Pipe it down a notch," she told her furry friends, who both wagged their tails at her.

Stone stepped up into the sleigh and tucked a large red woolen blanket across her legs. He didn't need the extra cover for himself, but he didn't complain when Felicity offered to share hers with him. Instead, he just smiled down at her, happy to be spending the day in such a fun way.

Stone threaded the reins through his fingers and clicked his tongue at the horses.

"Preach! Deke! Git up!"

The horses pulled forward and the sleigh lurched into motion. Felicity curled her hand through Stone's arm and leaned a little closer to him to maintain her balance.

"Sorry," he apologized, grinning down at her. "It's been a while since I've driven a team so I may need a brush-up course today."

It was more of a *sorry, not sorry* as far as he was concerned. He hadn't really meant for the sleigh to pitch forward the way it had, but he hadn't anticipated the unexpected benefits from the movement, either, especially when she'd scooted closer to him and didn't remove her hand from his arm even after they were well away from the barn.

But he wasn't going to tell her that.

"I used to drive the sleigh and the hay cart for Frost and Sharpe sometimes back when I was a teenager."

"I remember," she said without meeting his gaze.

"You do?" This revelation surprised him, because he barely remembered Felicity at all from his high school days. He'd known her as Sharpe's little sister but hadn't paid much attention to her.

"You seriously didn't know I had a crush on you?" She sounded genuinely surprised.

His gaze widened. "What?"

"Boys are so hopeless." This time she did meet his gaze, and her blue eyes were glinting with amusement.

"Wait, wait, wait. Before you start insulting my entire gender, let's go back to the crush part." He flashed her a cheeky grin. "I want to hear all about it."

"Yeah, you'd like that, wouldn't you? Stroke your already perpetually overinflated ego? I don't think so."

"Oh, come on," he said, guiding the Percherons down the lane and out into the woods, the sleigh bells jingling as merrily as his heart was feeling. "You brought it up. How did I not know you were crushing on me?"

"It's not as if it would have been obvious. Not to you, anyway. I was too shy to even speak to you, for starters. I always got tongue-tied whenever I was around you. But I was always aware when you were over at the farm hanging out with Sharpe. I was stealthy back then."

She let out a laugh that was almost a giggle and clapped a hand over her mouth in embarrassment.

"There was that time my friends and I ordered a pizza to be delivered to your house. Do you remember that ever happening?"

He threw back his head and roared with laughter. "All meat, which was great, but you ordered extra anchovies on it. Yuck! Believe me, I remember telling the delivery guy I hadn't ordered anything, and he'd given my exact name and address and said it was paid for so I might as well eat it. I had to pick off all the little fish. So—what other things do I not know about?"

"I'll admit to nothing else either positive or negative that may have impacted your life in any way. Or that you had no clue about at all. Otherwise, you're going to start to believe I'm a stalker."

"No. You weren't. Just a teenage girl, the same as any other, probably silly and giggly and full of drama, right? Oh man. Those were the days, huh? Don't you miss it? When we had our whole lives ahead of us, we thought we were going to conquer the world like no one else ever had? No worries other than what we were going to wear to impress the girls—or boys, in your case. Our only concerns were how to somehow pass all of our courses so we could graduate and how not to get caught whenever we decided to ditch class. I was so stupid about all that, though, going right across the street from the school to the burger joint where everyone could see me. Bright guy, right?"

"You certainly shone like a star on my radar."

He grinned down at her.

"Anyway, I don't remember middle and high school quite that way," she admitted thoughtfully. "I wouldn't go back to those extreme emotions and high school angst for all the money in the world. Feeling on the top of the world one moment and then as low as dirt the next. Ugh. No, thank you. I do remember working hard every day to prepare for college and being excited about the plans I was making for beyond high school, but other than that, while I did enjoy the academics, I didn't really like the social part of school all that much. I worked after school and on weekends here at the farm, so I didn't do many extracurricular activities, and I had only a handful of close friends. There were no letter jackets for me—mine or a boyfriend's."

"You actually liked school? Of course you did. I'm guessing you didn't ditch class once, did you, Miss Perfect?"

"I'm not anywhere close to perfect," she shot back at him.

He was only teasing her, but he felt as if he'd suddenly touched a nerve.

"As a matter of fact, I never did cut class. And yes, I enjoyed my studies. I worked hard and always turned in my homework on time."

"Teacher's pet," he teased, trying to make her smile.

It worked.

"Bad boy," she countered, tossing him a cheeky grin that made his heart pound faster. "And don't even try to deny it."

"I would never..."

Suddenly, Deke slipped on the icy path and the sleigh skidded sideways, nearly off the path.

Stone's attention immediately snapped back to the geldings and his knowledgeable gaze swept across both of the horses, observing the way they were standing.

"Whoa," Stone said, gently pulling back on the reins. "Easy there, boys. Easy, now. Whoa, boys."

"Stay put," he told Felicity as he grabbed a hoof scraper from the kit he always carried and hopped down from the sleigh. He usually drove with a vet kit just in case of injury. "I'll handle this."

He supposed it didn't really surprise him when Felicity totally ignored his advice to stay up on the sleigh and scrambled down after him, commanding the dogs to stay on the back seat and expecting them to actually listen to her.

The Percherons were standing still, chuffing as cold air met with their warm breaths and puffed from their nostrils. Stone ran a comforting hand down each of their muzzles, his experienced gaze carefully observing each horse for any signs of distress. It could be that one of them had merely slipped on black ice, but Stone felt in his gut it was more than that, and he never ignored his gut feelings, especially about horses, as most often he was right.

He watched the horses for a moment, speaking in a low, reassuring tone as he assessed them with a narrowed gaze.

Deke shifted his weight and that was when Stone spotted it.

The gelding was favoring his right front foot, not quite placing it down on the ice. Since Deke was harnessed to the right side, Stone was easily able to examine his leg. He reached for Deke's fetlock and applied gentle pressure so the horse would lift his foot. Likely, the horse had caught a rock or something under his hoof in his shoe. Stone pulled the scraper from his back pocket, but when he leaned Deke's leg on his knee so he could scrape underneath, Deke neighed in distress and tossed his head, pulling his leg away. Deke was a gentle gelding and never balked at having his feet looked at, which only added to Stone's concern.

"Easy, Deke. Easy, boy." Stone released Deke's leg and probed the tender fetlock with his fingers, noting when the generally sound, stable gelding suddenly chuffed and shifted, trying to get away from Stone's touch.

"Poor thing. Has he come up lame?" Felicity asked, placing a palm against the gelding's neck, and lowering her brow. "He really looks as if he's suffering."

"Looks like. I don't want to take him any farther on this leg. We'll need the vet to look him over to be sure what's going on here. He'll probably have to do an X-ray."

"Oh no," Felicity said, kissing Deke's muzzle. "You poor thing."

Stone started unhooking Deke from the sleigh without another word. There was no way Deke could pull the sleigh back to the barn and Stone wasn't even going to have him try.

"What's the plan now?" Felicity asked, moving around to stroke between Deke's ears and mutter gentle sweet nothings to him.

"I'll walk Deke back to the barn and call

the vet on the way. It'll have to be slow going, though. I don't want to hurt Deacon any more than he already is. Then I'll bring back the single harness for Preacher so we can return the sleigh to where it belongs."

"And while you're doing that, I'll stay here with Preacher and the dogs to keep them calm and safe."

It wasn't a question, but Stone winced and nodded anyway. It was exactly what he'd been about to suggest, as there really wasn't any other way.

"I'm sorry to have to ask this of you. I know it's freezing out here. I promise I'll be back as fast as I can."

"No worries," she said. "Except for poor Deke. You take good care of him, and we'll be fine out here."

Except Stone *was* worried. It was icy cold, and he was going to have to take it easy on Deke getting him back to the barn. It would be a long, cold wait for Felicity.

But what else could he do?

It *was* freezing, and by the time Stone finally returned with the single-horse harness looped over his broad shoulder, Felicity felt like a human ice cube. Her nose was numb, her cheeks felt as if she was experiencing dozens of little bee stings on them, and her fingers and toes hurt. She'd unharnessed Preacher and had thrown his blanket over him, then wrapped the woolen blanket that had come with the sleigh around her shoulders and brought Tugger and Dandy up with her. But even cuddling with the two furry dogs, she couldn't seem to maintain her warmth. She was huddled in the sleigh worrying about the approaching darkness when Stone arrived, jogging up the path as fast as he could.

She'd never been so happy to see anyone in her life.

"Finally," she exclaimed, relief flooding through her. "I was beginning to think I was going to have to spend the night here."

Stone's cheeks were red, and his chest was heaving with exertion.

"Sorry. I came back as quickly as I could. I knew you were out here freezing your nose off, but I had to let Sharpe and Frost know what was happening with Deke so they could inform the vet when he got there."

"No w-worries," she answered, but her teeth were chattering, and she couldn't stop them.

"Give me a second to get Preach harnessed and we'll be on our way," he promised, giving her a concerned once-over.

Felicity was grateful for his expertise with the horses, and she was equally thankful for his warmth. As soon as Stone crawled onto the seat of the sleigh, he put his arm around Felicity and drew her close to his chest in order to still her shivering. He clicked his tongue for Preacher to move out and in no time, they were on their way back to the barn, for the most part no worse for the wear than when they'd started.

When they approached the barn, Sharpe was pacing outside in the yard, his expression grim.

"What's the word on Deke?" Stone asked, hopping down from the sleigh, and then reaching up to help Felicity to the ground.

Sharpe didn't miss the gesture and briefly narrowed his eyes on them, but all of them had much more to worry about at the moment.

Felicity had been crawling on and off this sleigh since she was a kid, but right now she was bundled up very much like a bear ready for hibernation and was so cold and stiff from her long wait in the freezing weather she could barely move, so she was grateful for Stone's assistance.

"The vet's in with Deke now," Sharpe said.

"I'll go in and see him right away." Stone turned to Felicity and looked her over. "Why don't you run up to the main house and get warm?" he suggested, pressing a palm to her shoulder. "I'm sure they've got a good fire going in the woodstove. Get yourself some hot chocolate and hover near the stove for a while."

Once again, Sharpe looked suspiciously from one to the other. Felicity suddenly felt very much like the little sister and had to quell the urge to wriggle out of Stone's grasp.

With effort, she held her ground. No matter how she felt at the moment, she was a grown woman capable of making her own decisions and Sharpe needed to mind his own business. Besides, there was nothing going on between her and Stone except perhaps a growing friendship. Sharpe could take his nosiness and stick it in his ear.

"Stop stalling," she told both of the men.

"We're missing what's important here. Let's go find out what's happening with Deke."

Both of them stared at her wide-eyed.

"But—" Stone started, but she held him off from completing his statement with a flick of her mittened hand.

She headed for the barn, not looking back. Stone and Sharpe shared a glance and then followed her in.

She rushed to Deke's stall, where Frost and the town vet, Shannon McAllister, were bent over the gelding, examining Deke's leg. Felicity quietly entered the stall and knelt before the horse's head.

"How is he?" Felicity asked softly, running a reassuring hand down Deke's muzzle and letting the gelding know she was there for him.

"Nothing's broken," Shannon said, gently lowering Deke's foot to the ground. "I'll need to x-ray him, to be certain, but it looks to me as if he has a torn ligament."

Frost groaned. "Poor old guy. That's gotta hurt."

"Yes," Shannon agreed. "I'm going to put him on total stall rest—that means not even letting him out into the paddock. I'll provide anti-inflammatories and some pain medication to keep him comfortable."

The stall was already quite crowded with three people and a large draft horse, so Stone and Sharpe remained outside the stall, leaning on the door. Stone's gaze met Felicity's and he wordlessly offered her his support and encouragement. She nodded her understanding and wished the same for him. She knew how important horses were to him.

Frowning, a deep scowl heavy over his gray eyes, Frost patted Deke on the flank and exited the stall, gesturing with a jerk of his chin that Felicity should do the same.

"So we're down to one horse, then," Sharpe said in his usual practical, no-nonsense tone that got everyone's attention and pushed them forward toward what should happen next.

Felicity and Stone—and no doubt Frost, who took care of all the animals on the farm—were worried about Deke's health, whereas Sharpe's mind had already moved on to taking care of farm business.

Felicity's temper flared despite knowing Sharpe didn't mean anything by it. He wasn't being mean or coldhearted. It was just the way he was and always had been. She knew without a doubt he cared about Deacon's health and wellbeing. He just processed his emotions in a different way, by thinking about what would come next.

She didn't think her frustration with her brother showed in her expression, but Stone, who was standing next to her, shifted just enough to press his palm against the small of her back. No one else might have noticed, but he did, and perhaps he was telling her he felt the same way.

"We'll have to cut down on the number of rides each day, since Preach won't be able to keep up with our current schedule on his own. We don't want to overwork him and have him go lame, as well," Sharpe continued, his dark brow lowering. "That's going to cost us, as sleigh rides are one of our biggest draws."

"We knew this day was going to come for both of the geldings," Frost reminded Sharpe. "These old guys have worked hard for us all these years. They deserve a retirement where they can relax and spend their days out in the sunshine enjoying the grassy pasture. It's just that maybe that will be sooner rather than later."

Sharpe nodded and pressed his lips into a hard, straight line. Felicity was actually rather surprised he didn't argue the point. It was clearly a discussion they'd already had in the recent past, for him to actually be agreeing with Frost's assessment of the situation.

"There's a horse auction Friday at the Denver Coliseum Events Center I've had my eye on," Frost said. "I hadn't originally planned to attend, because I was hoping the Percherons would make it until spring before we had to change them out for a new team. But God clearly has something else in mind."

"We'll have to pivot," Sharpe agreed. "See where the Lord leads us."

He sighed and picked his cowboy hat off his head, brushing his palm back through his hair. "Frost and I will take a closer look at the offerings in the catalogue tonight and make a decision as to what we should do."

Suddenly his brow furrowed, and he shook his head. "Wait. That's not going to work."

"Why not?" Felicity asked.

"Frost and I have a business meeting with the county. It's important and we can't reschedule."

"Stone and I can go to the auction," Felicity suggested. "Problem solved."

She was no expert in choosing a good horse and wouldn't have the slightest clue what to look for other than if the horse was cute or not, or if she liked the coloring of it, or possibly if she made an emotional connection.

But Stone knew at least as much about horses as Frost did. He had a healthy respect and love for the animals. For a long time they'd been his livelihood. She had no doubt whatsoever he could pick out the best team for her brothers.

"We can't ask—" Sharpe started, but Stone interrupted him before he could finish his sentence.

"You're not asking. I'd be happy to do it. Just set us up with the details of the horses you're interested in looking at and we're on it. I'll keep my eye out for the finest horses for the best prices."

"Yeah, that might work. But you're sure you want to take Felicity with you? She might be more of a hindrance than a help," Sharpe said.

"Gee, thanks, bro," Felicity said, giving her brother a good shove.

Stone laughed. "I don't mind if your little sister hangs around. Maybe I can teach her a thing or two about horses during the auction."

Felicity eyed him, feeling as if she wanted to kick him in the shin.

After all, he deserved it, didn't he?

Chapter Six

Friday morning promptly at 5:00 a.m., Stone arrived at Winslow's Woodlands to pick up Felicity, a two-horse trailer attached to his pickup. It was a good two hours' drive to the Coliseum Events Center in Denver even without hauling a horse trailer behind him, which slowed things down a bit, especially on snowy mountain curves.

As far as Stone was concerned, it was oh-dark-thirty, and he could barely keep his eyes open. He'd never been a morning person, not even when he was a kid, and though he'd hooked up the horse trailer to the truck the night before, he'd still had to rise at four in the morning in order to shower so he would look presentable to Felicity. He'd even trimmed down his scruff and applied aftershave—kind of a silly thing to do when a man was going to spend the day in the dust at a horse auction, but there it was.

The truth was, he wasn't trying to smell good for the horses. That thought made him grin from ear to ear.

Felicity came out of the house carrying a large canvas bag over her shoulder and two travel mugs full of hot coffee. Stone hopped out of the cab and rushed around to open the passenger door and take the coffee mugs from her hands, passing them up to her after she was settled in the cab with her seat belt fastened.

As he put the truck in gear, she chirped, "Good morning," and handed him a mug of coffee.

He eyed her warily, lifting one eyebrow.

"You're a morning person," he accused.

"Guilty as charged." She chuckled, her gaze glittering with amusement. "I've always been a rise-and-shine kind of person."

"Why am I not surprised?" he grumbled good-naturedly. Waking up with the sun matched her personality perfectly.

"I take it you're a night owl?" she asked, turning in her seat.

"I always have been. Rodeos are most often held in the afternoons and evenings, which suited me just fine because that was when I was most coherent."

All the parties and his once-wild lifestyle had also been nighttime activities, but he thanked the good Lord every day for rescuing him from the pitfalls of that world. He could hardly believe that had ever been his life.

He'd take Felicity's morning cheerfulness any day of the week.

Felicity opened her canvas bag and pulled out a binder, flipping it open to the first page.

"This has the schedule for the auction and a list of all the available horses we can bid on," she said. "The auction starts at nine, but the doors open at seven thirty a.m. So we can walk around the basement level and observe all the horses."

"Did your brothers have any specific drafts in mind, or are they relying on us to use our best judgment to pick out a team?"

He hoped it was the latter so he could show off his skills when it came to selecting the best horses. He knew he could really do right by the Winslows if only he was given the opportunity to do so.

Felicity flipped forward a few pages and Stone could see the one listing that had been highlighted in fluorescent yellow.

Only one listing?

"My brothers were extremely specific, actually. There's a matched pair of Clydesdales they want us to bid on. They weren't really interested in anything else."

"Sounds good," Stone said, disappointment flooding through him. So Sharpe and Frost hadn't sent him to do a job any more complicated than bidding and hauling, after all. He wished they'd shown a little more trust in him, but there it was.

Felicity chatted happily throughout the drive and didn't appear to notice his mood had taken a nosedive. He was trying to stay cheerful and upbeat for her sake.

After all, he was spending the day with Felicity. He might as well enjoy it. And he'd always liked the thrill of auctions, the fast pace and trying to get the jump on any competition.

They arrived at the Events Center in Denver just after seven and refilled their coffee mugs at a coffee cart located on the mezzanine level.

The horses were cordoned off in the lower level. Since Felicity's brothers had already made the decision for them on which horses to bid for, they took their time strolling around, looking at a variety of horses—quarter horses for roping and cutting, and saddlebreds and thoroughbreds for sporting.

They eventually found the Clydesdales, whose coats had been brushed to a gleaming shine. Their manes and tails had been pleated and brightly ribboned.

Felicity appeared immediately delighted with the pair.

"They're gorgeous," she whispered up at Stone. "No wonder my brothers were so sold on these guys."

"Yeah," Stone agreed, but his gaze carefully traveled over each horse. Something in his gut was protesting that they weren't as great as they seemed. If only he could see what was bothering him.

He entered the cordoned-off area where the drafts stood.

"May I?" he asked the nearest handler, who crossed his arms and nodded his assent.

Stone looked into the horse's mouth, then ran his hands across the nearest Clydesdale's head, neck and back and then down each of his legs. He then turned to the other gelding and did the same, first spending extra time looking at his head and then carefully feeling down one of his front feet, gently pressing the area from the knee to the fetlock.

"Can we see this guy walk in the round pen?" Stone asked, pointing to the gelding he'd just been observing.

One of the ranch hands hanging out with the drafts took the Clydesdale in question to a nearby small round pen set up for just such evaluations.

Stone homed in on the animal, carefully observing his gait as he circled the pen at a walk, trot and canter.

"What is it?" Felicity asked softly. "Is something wrong?"

Stone shook his head, but he was unable to shake the feeling that the horse wasn't completely sound. "Not necessarily. It's more just a feeling I have."

"I trust your feelings," Felicity assured him.

"Thank you," he told the rancher. "Much appreciated for your time."

The two men shook hands and Stone drew Felicity away.

"I don't think they're going to work for Winslow's Woodlands," he told her. "We need to find out what other draft teams are here, so we have a backup plan in place just in case."

"Are you sure?" she asked, and then scoffed and waved away her own question. "No. Of course, you're sure. I'm glad you're here to ask the hard questions."

Still, she looked worried—not that Stone could blame her. Frost and Sharpe had been extremely specific in their choices, and they'd only made one. But they hadn't seen the actual horses as he had, and he had to follow his gut.

"I noticed many telltale signs that there might be an issue with one of the horses," he explained. "For example, when I was looking at the Clydesdale's face, I noticed his nostrils were tight and it appears he grinds his teeth. His eyes weren't bright, and I didn't make a good connection with him. His eyes were large as if startled by something and then his eyelids would droop. And while his ears weren't plastered all the way back on his head as when they are suddenly disturbed by something, they were flopping to the side and didn't stay upright. His posture wasn't quite right, either, and I noticed bite marks on his sides, though he'd been well-groomed to cover those."

He took a deep breath and let it out slowly, knowing he was talking too fast. "Most of all, though, I noticed the horse was shifting a lot. I believe I felt what were signs of ringbone on his pastern. I suspect, taking everything together, that we may have an unbalanced team."

"So he's out, then," Felicity said with a sigh.

"We won't know for sure until we see them pull a wagon in the arena, but I'm fairly certain what we're going to see—the first horse will be doing all the pulling while the second holds back, making the first one do all the work. It takes a close eye to notice it's happening, but we'll want the pair we select today to pull equally. Otherwise it's not fair to the one horse who does all the work."

Felicity removed her binder from her canvas bag and flipped it open. "Let's see what else we've got to look at in the way of draft teams."

Stone read over her shoulder as she went down the list, marking anything else either of them thought might work for Winslow's Woodlands.

There weren't a lot of choices when it came to matched draft pairs. There were a lot of quarter horses used by cowboys for herding and cutting, and other breeds more suited for jumping.

But drafts? Not so much. They just weren't used that much in the Denver metropolitan area, even in the rural areas.

"Let's check out these shires," Stone suggested, indicated a specific listing. "They're located at F4."

They walked to Row F and found the horses in question. Two jet-black shires—one gelding and one mare—were being tenderly groomed by an elderly farmer whose entire attention was on his horses.

"Oh dear," Felicity murmured under her breath, sounding discouraged.

Stone didn't have to guess as to why she was disheartened by the pair.

Unlike the Clydesdales with their shiny

coats and fancy plaits and ribbons, the shires looked like horses who'd been worked more than groomed.

But Stone had something to prove, both to Felicity and her brothers—and mostly to himself—and that started with this team of shires.

At this rate, it was going to be a very long day.

Felicity's heart fell. The Clydesdales had been so pretty. She'd instantly fallen in love with them and could easily picture them pulling the sleigh in winter and the hay cart in the summer. But she trusted that whatever Stone had seen was legitimate and they needed to look elsewhere. As he'd said, they wouldn't know for sure until they'd seen the horses pull a wagon in the arena.

But these black shires? She wasn't sure Frost and Sharpe were going to go for these two for a number of reasons. For one thing, they'd always liked showy horses where the sleigh ride was concerned, and these shires were anything but showy. And though she didn't know much about draft teams, she was fairly certain there was some kind of rule or something about not putting a gelding and a mare together.

She considered snapping a few pictures and messaging her brothers with them but hesitated, eventually deciding against it. She didn't want Sharpe and Frost to doubt Stone's capabilities, and that was exactly what would happen if Felicity started second-guessing what he was doing here.

As far as she was concerned, he'd proven himself with the Clydesdales. There weren't too many men who would have taken the time to make the observations he'd made, and in the long run he may have saved Winslow's Woodlands a lot of time and money.

Felicity introduced herself and Stone to the elderly farmer who only called himself Martin and shook hands with him.

"They're ten years old?" Stone asked, checking the horses' teeth, and running his palms across each of the shires to look for soundness, just as he'd done with the Clydesdales.

"They'll give you many long years of good service," Martin said. "That, I can promise you."

Felicity stood back from the exchange but

watched Stone and Martin interact. She was more of a people person than Stone was, but he had a job to do here that went far beyond the scope of Felicity's knowledge.

She closely observed Martin as he spoke of his animals.

"I'm proud of these two," Martin said, patting one of the horses' flanks. The farmer swallowed hard, and his eyes turned glassy as he spoke. Felicity sensed there was much more to the story. "They've served me well and they'll do the same for you."

"I'm sure you must be proud of them," she said. "They're a fine pair." She didn't really see anything particularly spectacular about them, but clearly the horses meant something special to him. Maybe it was more of a heart thing to the farmer.

And possibly Stone felt the same way. She was positive she saw a glimmer of interest in his eyes that had been missing when he'd been looking at the Clydesdales, or any other horses they'd seen that day, for that matter.

"Can I trouble you to walk these two beauties in the round pen?" Stone asked politely. Felicity noticed he was using a gentle but respectful tone different than his usual vigorous, raspy baritone. Had he also recognized the farmer's attachment to his horses and was trying to be kind?

Felicity thought so, and admiration swelled up in her heart.

Stone and Martin led the two shires into the round pen, and then one by one Stone put them through their paces around the corral, starting at a walk and then moving them through their paces—trotting and cantering. A full gallop would have been too much for the large horses in the small space, but Stone evidently saw what he was looking for.

He let out a low whistle, his eyes shining with fascination.

Felicity found it interesting that in the short time she and Stone had spent together, she could already read his expressions. And right now he was about to jump out of his boots with excitement.

"Look at their gaits," Stone said over a breath. "Absolutely beautiful. These two are truly remarkable."

He winked at Felicity and turned to the farmer, shaking hands with the old man.

"I know exactly why you feel as you do about your shires. These two are magnificent. Felicity and I will be bidding on them today, and if we win, I promise we'll take the very best care of them possible."

Martin's eyes turned misty. Felicity wondered if Stone understood just how important his words had been to the elderly farmer. She suspected he did.

"Aye," Martin said. "It kills me to even be here today. These two have been my partners many a day. I wouldn't be selling them except…" He paused and sniffed. "My wife has cancer, and the insurance we have isn't paying the bills. A man's got to do what a man's got to do."

"I'm so sorry," Felicity said, laying a hand on the farmer's arm. "Cancer is a terrible thing. We'll be praying for your wife and you."

"My mama is also fighting that fight. It's awful. We wish you and your wife every blessing. And again, I promise your horses will have the best home we can give them," Stone assured him.

"That was really sweet of you," she said as she and Stone headed upstairs for the auction.

"What's that?" Stone asked, wrapping his

arm across her shoulders so they wouldn't be separated by the pushing crowd.

"The way you treated that farmer back there. He's really suffering, having to give his beloved horses away, and you treated him with such respect and care. I can't imagine how hard it must be for him to part with Jack and Jill."

Stone's brow lowered. "I hate cancer so much."

Felicity placed her palm over his heart as they walked. "I know you do. I feel the same way."

"We've got to win those shires, no matter what. I'll put my own money in if I have to, thought I doubt it will be necessary. But for Martin's sake…"

"You'd do that?"

Stone's jaw hardened and he nodded. He wouldn't share how he was feeling with her, of course, always wanting to appear the tough guy, but Felicity suspected he was struggling with strong emotions of his own. This whole thing was hitting far too close to home.

"Yes," she agreed. But she had to ask. "Do you think Frost and Sharpe will be okay with this purchase? They aren't going to freak out when you bring shires home instead of the Clydesdales?"

He glanced down at her in surprise. Whatever else was on his mind, it wasn't that. "Sure. Why wouldn't they be? We're going to get those two shires for a song. Most bidders are going to look right past them because the farmer hasn't had the time to keep them up properly."

"But you're sure they're sound."

"Better than sound. They have beautiful gaits and will look gorgeous hooked to the front of the sleigh. They just need a little work, is all. Give them extra oats and comb out the knots in their manes and tails and they'll look every bit as good as the Clydesdales. Better, even."

"I heard somewhere that you're not supposed to pair a gelding and a mare, though. Is that something Sharpe and Frost will be concerned about?"

He scoffed. "If it is, it shouldn't be. That's just an old wives' tale. Some of the best pairs are gelding-mare teams. And you could see Jack and Jill belong together."

Felicity believed Stone, and she trusted him. How could she not, with the way his blue eyes shone with exhilaration? He really believed what he said. But she wasn't as sure about her brothers. They could be pretty stiff-necked when they wanted to be.

But Stone and Sharpe had been best friends since childhood. Surely Stone would know Sharpe's personality better than anyone?

She just had to believe it would all work out for the best in the end.

Wouldn't it?

Chapter Seven

Despite the fact that he'd risen so early the day before, Stone woke up with the sun, anxious to get over to Winslow's Woodlands so he could see everyone. He and Felicity had arrived back late the evening before from the Events Center in Denver, and hadn't seen Frost and Sharpe when they'd unloaded the shires into the Winslows' barn. He couldn't wait to talk to them about their new drafts, which Stone and Felicity had managed to grab at a major steal, as they'd been the only ones bidding on the beautiful pair of shires.

Stone had slipped in a little extra of his own money when Felicity wasn't looking. He felt it was the least he could do to properly compensate the poor farmer. It probably wouldn't go far in paying for cancer specialists, but at least it was something.

As he'd suspected, there weren't many bidders looking for a draft pair, and those who were had had their eyes turned by the fancy Clydesdales with their plaited and ribboned manes, rather than the fairy knots the shires wore.

But Stone knew what he could do with these shires far outweighed the ridiculous price for which the Clydesdales had eventually gone.

Despite the early morning, when he pulled up next to the barn at Winslow's Woodlands, Frost already had the shires out in the corral, and Sharpe and Felicity were leaning on the fence watching their brother put the gelding through his paces.

He could hardly wait to talk to Felicity's brothers about his amazing purchase, but as he approached, he immediately noticed Felicity's expression. Her lips were curled down, and her gaze flickered with—what? Anger? Frustration? Disappointment?

She lowered her eyes and gave a faint shake of her head.

Sharpe turned as soon as he heard Stone's

footsteps approaching. If Felicity had been warning Stone off, this was why. His friend was most definitely ticked off.

"It's about time you got here," Sharpe snapped. "We've been waiting for you."

"Why?" Stone asked, not even beginning to be able to guess what was up with his friend. He'd learned a long time ago not to read too much into Sharpe's moods. Sharpe was his best friend, but he had a way about him that perfectly matched his name. He was—edgy.

Frost approached and tipped off his hat to scrub his fingers through his blond hair. "You want to explain yourself about these two?"

Felicity crossed her arms and scowled. Stone couldn't tell whether she was piqued at him or at her brothers, but he hoped it was the latter.

"How do you mean?" Stone asked.

"Unless my eyes have gone bad, those aren't the Clydesdales Sharpe and I sent you after. Not even close."

Stone frowned and squared his shoulders. It was bad enough that his friends were all over him about his "mistake" without Felicity being here to witness this humiliation.

"I can explain." Stone thought they owed him at least that much. Couldn't they just listen to him?

"Knock it off with the attitude, you two," Felicity snapped, glaring at her brothers. "Let Stone speak."

So she was with him, then. For some reason that boosted Stone's confidence and he felt a couple of inches taller.

"Believe me, you didn't want to pay what those Clydesdales ended up going for. In their case, pretty only went skin-deep."

"They weren't sound," Felicity added. "One of the horses was lagging and making the other do all the pulling."

"Oh, as opposed to…*these*?" Sarcasm oozed from Sharpe's voice. "They look like they just came off a farm. A *real* farm."

"As a matter of fact, they did. These sweethearts here just need some elbow grease and a little bit of good feed for their natural glow to reappear," Felicity said, echoing what Stone had told her the previous day.

That might have helped his cause had she not continued.

"Jack and Jill were owned by this poor farmer whose wife is suffering with cancer. It broke his heart to have to part with this pair, and he only sold them because he needed to pay for his wife's care."

Oh boy. Stone tensed for the response.

Sharpe rolled his eyes and groaned. "Stone...*please* tell me you didn't let her talk you into buying these shires based on some sob story from an old farmer?"

It was all Stone could do not to deck his best friend, for not trusting his expertise with horses, but mostly for insulting his sister. But he needn't have worried. Felicity lurched forward and punched Sharpe hard in the arm.

"Don't be mean. This isn't about me. Stone knows what he's doing, and he would never pick up a bad team just because of a story—*any* story."

Stone could see he was getting in between the siblings, and he didn't like the feeling it gave him.

This was exactly why he could never date Felicity, no matter how much he'd grown to like her. He never wanted to make her choose between him and her family like she seemed to be doing right now.

It was a good reminder of what was what in the world, and he took a gigantic mental step backward.

"This pair will be great for you, I promise," Stone said. "Like Felicity said, the outside may need a little polish, but the inside is what really counts. Have you seen their gaits yet?"

"I was about to check them out around the corral," Frost said.

"Proof's in the pudding," Stone said, forcing a smile.

He leaned against the fence to watch Frost put Jack through his paces. Felicity leaned up next to him, resting one foot on the lower fence pole and nudging his shoulder with hers. When he glanced down at her, she smiled up at him encouragingly.

"Just ignore them," she whispered. She continued under her breath, "They're just being brats. They know perfectly well you would have picked the Clydesdales if they had been the best choice. They'll be thanking you by noon today for your judgment."

"Yeah, well…" he said.

He could overlook Sharpe's and Frost's

wrestling and teasing. He'd been doing it for years. Regular guy stuff.

It was Felicity he was having a tough time ignoring.

Felicity had spent Saturday afternoon and part of Sunday after church with the shires, brushing them to a sheen and using detangler to untangle the fairy knots and brush their manes and tails out.

They were a bit underweight, but nothing a solid diet couldn't fix, and they looked a hundred times better after a little bit of grooming.

Now that it was Monday, she was really starting to notice a difference in Jack and Jill. Their coats were already starting to buff to a sheen. Let her brothers complain *now* and see where it got them.

She still couldn't believe she'd had to step in between Stone and her brothers and stick up for him. Stone was Sharpe's best friend, and it made her so angry that they had put her in that awkward position of having to defend him in the first place. Better than anyone, they ought to know what a good guy Stone was.

After putting all the grooming tools away, she went to find Stone. She'd left him with five large bins of Winterfest decorations, telling him to put everything up any way he liked.

But when she approached the gift shop, she nearly had a heart attack. Stone was lying on his stomach on the roof, half dangling off it as he stapled silver and gold icicle lights to the edge of the eaves.

One leg was up while he gripped the shingles with his other foot. One wrong move and he was going to take a nosedive and probably break his neck.

Why wasn't he using a ladder like a normal person? Where was his common sense?

Her pulse jumped into overdrive as she dashed forward, thinking it was better that he see her first before she started yelling at him and take the chance of startling him into falling off the roof.

He grinned and waved when he saw her, his entire body shifting and making Felicity's breath hook.

"What on earth do you think you're doing?" she demanded, planting her fists on her hips and glaring up at him.

He looked at her in surprise, his brow rising and mouth gaping.

"I'm decorating for Winterfest, just like you asked me to do. Or at least I was trying to. What? You don't like the icicle lights across the eaves of the gift shop? I thought they'd look nice here. Give it a wintry feel, you know?"

"The lights look nice," she admitted, sighing in exasperation under her breath. "What I *don't* like is you dangling off the roof so recklessly, as if you don't have a care in the world. Haven't you ever heard of a ladder?"

"A ladder is way too much of a hassle. You have to keep going up and down and moving it around every five seconds. Up here on the roof I can move around freely from spot to spot."

"You are *dangling* off the roof," she repeated, exasperated by his clear lack of comprehension. "One wrong move and you'll roll right off."

He performed what looked to Felicity like a pushup on the roof until he was on his hands and knees. Then he sat back on his heels and rested his palms on his thighs.

"You're making too much of this. It's really no big deal, Felicity. I'm being careful."

"It's reckless," she snapped irritably. She knew she was being overdramatic. He probably was perfectly safe, but she was fighting off a sense of terror even she didn't quite understand. There was no way she was going to be able to explain her feelings to Stone.

"Please. Just get down from there."

"I only have two more yards to put up and then I'll be down," he promised her with a reassuring grin.

She turned away from him. She just couldn't watch him hanging over the eaves that way. Her gut churned.

Stone may have found the Lord and turned over a new leaf in his life, but in her opinion, he hadn't quite rid himself of his rash behavior, and the adrenaline rush that accompanied it. She supposed that would be something he would carry with him all through his life.

Stone had once chased that adrenaline rush on the back of a horse. And by goofing around with his friends on motorcycles. Now he had to find new ways to seek that thrill.

She should have known this would eventually happen, and that it would affect her this way. She had put on blinders and allowed herself to grow close to Stone as they worked together every day at Winslow's Woodlands. But all that time, she'd known the kind of man he was.

She even recognized the truth of her emotions, if only in her own heart. She was starting to develop feelings for her high school crush—*real* feelings, this time, and not silly teenage angst. But this was a good reminder that leaning into such emotions was nothing short of foolish.

She turned back when she heard Stone cheer.

"All done, and I plugged it in so you can see how it looks. I think it's pretty good. What do you think, Felicity? Woo-hoo!"

He cupped the edge of the eave with both hands and did a front flip forward off the roof. One of his hands slipped and for a moment he dangled in midair before he fell, as if in slow motion, into the evergreen bushes below him.

"Stone!" she cried in dismay, rushing toward him.

"Ow," he groaned, gingerly and tentatively

testing movement in his arms and legs and momentarily clutching his elbow.

"Nothing's broken," he assured her, laughing.

She slapped his shoulder with her open palm. "Crawl out of those bushes this minute and then we'll see how many of your bones are broken, you jerk."

His face turned bright red as he tried to stifle his laughter, but another chuckle escaped him, nonetheless. His eyes were glittering with amusement.

"You think this is funny?" she demanded, fighting the urge to shake him.

He grinned. "Kinda. Yes. You should have seen your face when I was dangling there."

"Don't you dare! I—I—" Suddenly her feelings overwhelmed her, and she whirled away from him, sinking to the ground and wrapping her arms around her legs with her eyes pressed into her knees so he couldn't see her cry.

"Hey," he said, crouching beside her and putting his arm around her. "What's wrong? What happened just now? I know you were ticked at me for being up on the roof, but I thought you were only teasing, or else I never would have performed a stunt like that. I was never in any danger, I promise."

She shook her head, wishing she could shake off her emotions just as easily. "Sorry I freaked out on you. Sometimes it's too much for me."

"Clearly I'm the one who should be apologizing," Stone countered, tucking a stray strand of her hair behind her ear. "You know I was only goofing around with you, right? I might do dumb stuff but not anything that would seriously put me in harm's way."

"I know." Felicity wished she could just dash her tears away and laugh it off, but it simply wasn't that easy to do. And the truth was, she wasn't entirely convinced Stone wouldn't put himself in jeopardy if it looked like something fun to do.

"Where did you put that box of silver and gold ribbons?" she asked, as if the past few minutes hadn't even happened. "I think they'd look really pretty on the shelves inside the gift shop."

"I put that bin on the front counter," he said, his brow furrowed in concern. "But—"

"Great." She cut him off. "Let's get going, then." Without another word, she rolled to her feet and led him into the gift shop, approaching the counter and rifling through the bin full of ribbons, untangling them and separating them into piles of silver and gold.

"What we're going to do is thread these ribbons throughout the merchandise on the shelves. Make it look good, but make sure customers can still easily see and get to all the merchandise."

Glass shelf modules were placed around the floor in the middle of the gift shop and were covered with candles and local merchandise, some specific to Winslow's Woodlands and some souvenirs for Colorado in general. Handmade wooden shelves made by Sharpe lined the walls and carried a number of different types of clothing from T-shirts to hoodies for all ages, along with a few clothing racks in the corners of the room.

"Show me," Stone said in a subdued voice. It also appeared he was holding back on speaking, for which she was glad. Right now, she wouldn't have been able to handle him pushing her on why her emotions were so on edge when she couldn't even explain it herself.

She grabbed a handful of silver and gold

ribbons and threaded them around the candle display.

"The shelves always look so barren after I've taken out the Christmas decorations, so I'm grateful for Winterfest."

"Any special way you want me to do this?" he asked, grabbing ribbons of his own and moving over to the clothing shelves.

"There's no right or wrong in this," she assured him. "Just whatever looks good."

He followed her lead, decorating the clothing shelves and tying some of the ribbons on the clothing racks.

"We could dangle some of these curlier ribbons off the ceiling beams," he suggested, wariness in his tone. "They'd look like snow falling."

"You'd use a ladder to hang them?"

"Yes, of course. And I'll be careful," he assured her. "I promise. You can even supervise me if you want."

She hesitated. "You're right. It would look good. None of this," she said, waving her arm between her and Stone, "is about you."

He crossed his arms, his full attention on her. "How do you mean?"

"Remember I told you about Trevor?" She

wasn't sure she wanted to get into this, but it was the only way for Stone to understand where she was coming from, so she continued.

"Yeah. Your last boyfriend. The guy who wouldn't make a commitment to you. The one who lost his life in that horrible avalanche."

"Trevor shouldn't have been where he was. He had no business snowboarding on that mountain. He was reckless and only thought about himself."

"Ah," Stone breathed. "And because of what you've seen, you think I'm the same way."

"Not exactly the same," she admitted. "You're definitely more mature than Trevor ever was, and you think of other people before yourself. But you're enough of a risktaker to worry me."

"Like, for example, when I was dangling off the roof like a goofball."

"Exactly."

"I was totally in control there, you know. There wasn't ever anything to worry about."

"Maybe that's how you saw it. Me, not so much."

"Okay, so it's a no-go for hanging the ribbons on these beams."

"I didn't say that. It's a good idea and they'll make the gift shop look especially festive. I just want you to be careful and not take unnecessary chances."

He held up his right hand, palm out. "From now on, I promise I will always look before I leap."

"It's not fair to ask that of you. You've chased adrenaline since you were a kid and it's part of your nature. It's not my place to tell you what to do and what not to do. Like I said, it's my issue, not yours."

"That doesn't mean I can't be aware of what might trigger you," he said. "And make sure I don't do anything to accidentally set you off."

"I have a ladder in the back room," she said. "Why don't you go get it and we'll hang these ribbons together."

She didn't want to talk about her triggers. She wanted to get this job done so she could make an early night of it and spend the evening alone in her room sorting through her emotions where no one could see her tears.

With her helping tape the ribbons and

handing them up to Stone, it took them no time at all to decorate the ceiling beams, and she had to admit the final effect was worth the effort. It was as if the gift shop had turned into a snowy, sparkly woodland.

Suddenly the bell over the door rang and both of them turned to see Sharpe entering. There was still tension between the three of them. Felicity felt it herself and could see it in Stone, whose jaw hardened as he stepped off the ladder and faced her brother.

Sharpe blew out a low whistle. "This place looks great. The customers will be enthralled when they come in here. It's as if the snow-fall has come inside."

Felicity let out the breath she'd been hold-ing and smiled at her brother. "You like it? It was Stone's idea. I never would have thought of it."

"Huh. Who would have thought Stone had a decorative bone in that thick head of his?" Sharpe grinned at his best friend.

"Hey," Stone protested, though he smiled, as well.

"Anyway," Sharpe continued, "I came up to congratulate you, Stone. After all the work you put in on the shires this weekend, I can already really see the difference. I don't know how you managed to get those fairy knots out of their manes and tails, though. It must have taken hours. They look so much better, and I had the opportunity to really check their gaits. You were right to have bid on them."

"But I didn't—" Stone started. Felicity briefly shook her head to cut off the rest of his sentence.

"I'm glad to hear it," Stone said instead. "I could see such potential in them despite the way they looked on the lot."

Sharpe grabbed a candy bar and a soda and tossed a couple of dollars onto the counter, then left as fast as he'd come in.

"You want to tell me what that was all about?" Stone asked. "Why was he praising me up, down and sideways? That isn't like him."

"It would be easier to show you. I've spent the last couple of days with the horses, grooming them and cleaning them up. They still need extra oats to get to a good weight, but they look a lot better than they did before. They just needed a little tender loving kindness."

Felicity turned the sign on the gift shop door to Be Back Soon and locked it behind her, leading Stone to the barn where the draft horses were kept. He walked close to her but kept his hands in the front pockets of his jeans, almost as if creating distance between them.

Felicity felt it. But what did she expect? She'd just pretty much insulted his entire lifestyle, pushing him away from her the way she had. But fair or not, that was how she felt, and she couldn't just ignore it whenever he did something reckless.

Stone let Felicity lead the way into the barn, but he was first inside Jack's stall, walking around the animal, his mouth agape.

"Is this even the same shire we bought the other day?" he said with a low whistle. "I don't even believe what I'm seeing."

"You know it is. Back at the auction, you looked right through a little dirt and knotted mane and tail to see what the horses really had to offer."

"This is amazing. You did a lot of work here to get them looking this good. How many hours of grooming did you put in?"

"Well, as I said, it was only a matter of

elbow grease. I bathed them and brushed their coats clean and then used cowboy detangler to work out the fairy knots in their manes and tails. It wasn't as bad as it looked. And anyway, I enjoy grooming horses. I've loved horses since I was a little girl, and it gave me the opportunity to spend some time with these two and bond with them."

"You're really something, you know that?" Stone grinned at her. "You even impressed Sharpe, and trust me on this one—that's hard to do."

Felicity felt herself flush from the toes of her boots to the roots of her hair.

Because she hadn't been trying to impress Sharpe.

She'd been trying to impress Stone.

Chapter Eight

❧

Stone spent the rest of the week going back and forth between offering guests sleigh rides with the new shires and helping Felicity in the gift shop. He'd been looking forward to Friday all week, since Felicity had promised they'd start working with the dogs on avalanche scent training. Having spent some time with Dandy, he really wanted to work with him again as a team.

After the whole incident with his foolhardy antics on the roof, he was more than a little worried Felicity might be triggered by avalanche scent work and decide not to do it, but if there was one thing he'd learned about her, it was that she was a strong and determined woman. When she decided to do something, it got done.

And who knew? Maybe this was a way of working through her grief over Trevor.

He just knew that he was excited about the opportunity to work with the dogs again, and to learn more about how service dogs helped people. Having seen dog therapy was one thing, but his adrenaline really kicked in at the thought of avalanche rescue training. When he'd heard how it was done, he'd practically begged Felicity to allow him to go along.

"I'm grateful my sister Molly is covering the gift shop for me today so we can get some coaching done. We'll be working inside the training center today," she informed him.

"What? I thought we were going to be working in the snow." How could they do avalanche work without being outside?

"Slow down there, cowboy," she said, chuckling. "We'll get there. I know you want to climb up on that bucking bronco and see if you can score your eight seconds, but you have to learn how to ride at a walk before you start galloping."

Curious, he followed her into the training building. Dandy and Tugger were already inside, running loose and play-wrestling with each other. The din of their barking echoed throughout the building, sounding quite a bit louder than their normal yips.

When Dandy saw Stone, he came at him at a full run, woofing his excitement and wagging his tail madly as he launched himself into Stone's arms and licked his face, apparently undeterred by his scruffy cheeks.

Stone laughed heartily as he scrubbed Dandy's ears with his fingers and kissed his snout. "I missed you, too, buddy."

Felicity joined in the laughter and then clapped a hand over her mouth and shook her head.

"Oh my. I'm so sorry. He was absolutely *not* supposed to do that."

"What? Welcome me to work?"

"Jump on people like that. If you weren't as big a man as you are, he would have knocked you down on your back."

"I kinda like it," he said, holding the dog in his arms. "It's like being welcomed with a big, furry hug. It makes me feel wanted."

"Well, then, we'll need to train Dandy to greet you that way only when you've commanded him to do so, and never to jump up on anyone else *ever*."

"Yeah," Stone agreed, planting another noisy kiss on the dog's ear. "I'd like to have something just between the two of us. That's a cool idea."

"We'll do that then as part of your training together. But we're going to start the morning with basic obedience," she told him.

"I thought Dandy already knew all of that stuff. He's been here at the training center for a while, hasn't he?"

"He has been, and he does know all his basic commands," she agreed with a cheeky grin. "This training is for you."

He widened his gaze on her. He couldn't decide if she was being serious or if she was just kidding. But the smile on her face indicated her true feelings and he winked back at her, letting her know he was man enough to take the joke.

"Before you know it, you'll have me sitting, staying and coming when you call," he teased, putting up his hands like paws and panting with his tongue lolling out to the side.

She shook her head and rolled her eyes at his goofiness.

She fitted Dandy with his red service vest,

then threaded a lime-green nylon martingale slip collar over the Lab's head. She clasped a leash on it and handed the other end to Stone. Then she gave him a nylon bag full of liver treats to clip to his belt.

"Dandy is primarily toy oriented, but we're going to start with food and a clicker to get him to focus. He's a wonderful worker, but he's still young and can be easily distracted. Dandy has to keep his attention completely on you while you're working together. You don't want his mind wandering when he's supposed to be finding a victim in the snow."

"Right," Stone agreed. He had some familiarity with basic dog commands but was glad she was giving him a brush-up.

"What you're going to do first is call Dandy's name and then reward him with a click and a treat the moment his eyes meet yours. The clicker is so he knows the exact moment he did what you wanted him to do, and the food is the follow-up reward. The goal is for him to look at you every single time you say his name."

"Easy enough," Stone said confidently. "Dandy. Dandy. Dandy. Dandy. Look at me, boy. Dandy. Dandy."

"Whoa, whoa, whoa." Felicity threw her hands into the air and giggled. "Slow down there, cowboy."

"What?" he asked, tilting his chin as he looked down at her. "You said to say his name."

"It's good that you're getting him excited. That's what we want—to put him into overdrive. To dogs, their jobs are playing with their trainers. So your energy flows through the leash from you to him. However…"

Stone snickered. He'd known that word was coming.

"You want Dandy to be immediately obedient to you. He should follow your command the first time you utter it, every time, which is why you don't want to ply him with his name over and over again like you just did. Say it once and wait until he focuses on you. Then, immediately reward him with a click and a treat."

Stone was at least as excited as Dandy was, but he labored to control his own enthusiasm as he worked on Dandy's focus throughout the room. Felicity then moved to having Dandy heel at Stone's left side and sit whenever he stopped, both leashed and without a lead.

They then worked on sit/stay and down/stay, all of which Dandy had already been well trained on. As Felicity had said, it was more about Stone and Dandy working together and becoming comfortable as a team.

When lunchtime arrived, they stopped and shared sandwiches Felicity provided. They sat across from each other at the desk in the corner of the room while Dandy and Tugger had some outdoor time as a break of their own.

"I thought the basics were going to be boring, but you made it fun," Stone said, biting into his tuna salad sandwich and then popping a chip into his mouth, followed by a long swig from his bottle of water.

"It's what you put into it," she said. "Everything is always easier when it's fun."

Stone paused, thinking not so much of the dog training today but to his future and what he would put into it.

"That's the attitude I want to bring to my new job, when I'm the instructor and not the student."

"Your new job?"

"In Wyoming. I think I told you about it. I'll be one of the instructors at a rodeo school. I'm super excited about it. I'll probably be working with younger kids, which is something I think I'll really enjoy doing. I was just considering how to harness their natural enthusiasm the way you do with the dogs."

Once, the thought of working with kids would have scared him, and he supposed in a way it still did. But after having interacted with the children at the avalanche shelter, he had a whole new perspective on how important it was to reach kids' hearts.

Felicity had stopped chewing, but she didn't interject with her own thoughts, so he kept talking.

"I don't know," he continued. "I suppose I'll find out how it goes when I get there."

"I think you'll be a great teacher," she assured him, but he didn't think her smile quite reached her eyes, and he wondered why.

He knew that he wasn't nearly as enthused about moving to Wyoming as he'd been months ago, when he'd first been considering it. At that time it had felt like the obvious next step since he'd never be a bareback bronc rider in pro rodeo again.

Yet, he was enjoying his time here at Winslow's Woodlands, and especially spending time with Felicity, more than he ever could have imagined he would, and he suddenly wasn't in any hurry to leave.

But he may as well get used to the fact that sooner or later his temporary position would come to completion, and he would be leaving.

He would climb that mountain when he came to it—no matter how hard that would be.

Felicity hadn't forgotten Stone's plans to eventually move to Wyoming and be a rodeo instructor, but she had pushed it to the back of her mind. He was here to support his mother, so she figured he'd be around for a while yet, and she intended to enjoy and appreciate every moment she could spend with him.

Yes, her heart ached just a little bit at the thought of him leaving, but there wasn't anything she could do to change that. It was just that they'd become such good friends in all the time they'd been working together, and in truth it was hard to imagine him moving on and not seeing his handsome smile every day. He would definitely leave a hole in her life when he left.

"Are you ready to do some more indoor work with Dandy?" she asked Stone, who'd just finished up his second sandwich. "We've got a lot more work to do today."

"Doesn't he get bored with sit, stay, down?" Stone asked.

Felicity laughed. "Dogs are always eager to work with their people. Everything is a game to them. I think it sounds more as if *you* are bored with sit, stay, down."

"Guilty as charged. Going over commands a few times is one thing, but this constant repetition is getting to me."

"As it happens, we're done with basic commands and will be moving on to games I think you'll find are more fun for *you*."

"Cool beans," he said, enthusiastically standing and stretching.

She chuckled and shook her head. The big goof. Who said *cool beans* anymore?

She was pleased that what they'd be working on this afternoon would actually be quite fun for both Stone and Dandy just as she'd told him. And it would be entertaining for her as well, as she watched the two of them play together.

Felicity called Dandy inside and vested him back up again, so he'd know it was time to go to work. She handed Stone one of the dog's favorite toys, a stuffed raccoon that squeaked whenever Dandy chewed on it. It was well-worn but perfect for what she wanted to use it for today.

"You're going to go to the far end of the room, where I've set up a variety of obstacles." She pointed to the area where she'd placed tipped-over chairs, tables, colorful boxes and even a huge pillow fort. "At the same time, I'll take Dandy to the other end of the room. When I tell you to go, I want you to get his attention and make sure he's wound-up about catching the raccoon. Then I'm going to distract Dandy and turn him around while you hide the toy."

"Sounds fun, just like you said."

"Oh, it is. When you're ready, you'll call Dandy to you and continue revving up his drive to find his toy—with one caveat. Try the best you can to not give him any indication, either verbally or with body cues, as to where you've hidden the raccoon. Let him do the hard work and sniff it out. And make sure you use the word *find* so he gets used to hearing that command."

Stone's smile split his face and Felicity could tell he was enjoying the event at least as much as Dandy.

The first time through, Stone barely hid the toy at all, leaving it right behind a tipped-over chair. When Felicity indicated the time was right, he called to the dog.

"Come on, Dandy. *Find.* Find your toy," he called in an excited, high-pitched voice. "Where's your raccoon?"

Dandy knew this game and immediately ran across the room, snuffling around Stone's heels before moving into work mode, his nose leading him around all of the obstacles in search of his toy.

It only took him seconds to find the raccoon, which he then tossed at Stone before sitting before him.

"Go ahead and play tug-of-war with Dandy for his reward," Felicity instructed. "And be sure and tell him what a good boy he is."

They ran the event a few more times, each time making it harder and harder for Dandy. Stone found newer and increasingly clever places to hide the toy, until in the last go-round, he hid the raccoon under a few cushions in the pillow fort.

This time when Stone called for Dandy to find his raccoon, the dog sniffed around for some time but came up empty.

"What do we do now?" Stone asked, running his fingers through the red-gold hair at his neckline. "He doesn't seem to be able to find it. Should I show him where it is?"

"No, not yet. Now it's time for you to become a team. Walk him around all the obstacles and command him to *find*. You can indicate where you want him to look by pointing to an obstacle, but let his nose take the lead."

"Come on, Dandy. *Find*. Where's your raccoon? Is it over here?" He pointed toward an empty yellow crate.

Dandy sniffed and immediately turned away, looking back at Stone for further directions.

Watching the man-and-dog team work together brought a lump of emotion to Felicity's throat. Training dogs had long been a part of her life, ever since her high school days, but seeing Stone's enthusiasm with Dandy brought everything she'd experienced to date in dog training to a whole new level.

At length, Dandy scratched at the pile of cushions and then dived into it, successfully retrieving the raccoon. He pranced around with the toy between his teeth, shaking it and growling as Stone grabbed one end and the two played tug-of-war together.

"Next, we're going to move from scenting toys to sniffing out humans by using Sharpe's old sweater." She handed him the sweater in question, a tattered old thing. "It's the same idea as the raccoon, and Dandy will immediately recognize Sharpe's scent."

Stone wrinkled his nose. "You think?"

Felicity laughed. "I meant his human scent. As you've no doubt noticed, dogs have a much higher capacity for smell than people do. They can sniff out bombs, fruit and drugs, among other things, and can even smell changes in a diabetic's blood sugar level."

She gestured down to Dandy. "That's why they're so great at search and rescue. Many more lives are saved with the use of K9s in the field. Search and rescue is a serious business, but at the end of the day, to Dandy it's just a game, and one he's good at. Are you ready to play Find Sharpe's Sweater?"

Stone nodded enthusiastically. "This I've got to see."

Chapter Nine

Stone sniffed at Sharpe's sweater and shook his head, looking as if he were about to sneeze. "Forget scenting out a human. Dandy ought to be able to find this sweater just based on Sharpe's aftershave. It's not so bad on this sweater, but I remember back in high school he'd overkill on the woodsy aftershave." Finding that sweater ought to be a piece of cake for Dandy.

"Oh, Stone," Felicity said, pressing her palm to his bicep as she broke out in laughter. "I can't believe you'd say such a thing about your best friend."

"You think I'm kidding?"

"No. I don't doubt you in the least. Thankfully, he's toned it down over the years. I guess he's not quite so anxious to impress the ladies anymore. Or else he finally figured out he smells woodsy even without aftershave, given that he runs the tree farm."

"You said it's the same idea as the toy?"

"More or less. Play a little tug-of-war to get him used to the scent and then hide it for him to find."

Stone ran through the exercise three times, making each one harder than the last, and always praising Dandy when he found the sweater.

He understood why Dandy did so well with the whole praise and a pat-on-the-head thing—Stone's ego swelled in his chest every time Felicity told him what a good job *he* was doing. He tried even harder because he knew she was watching him and he deeply desired to earn her metaphorical pats on the head.

"Now we're going to play another game you're both going to like," Felicity said. "Grab as many of those pillows and cushions as you can and put them in a pile right here." She pointed directly in front of her.

"Now what?" he asked, observing the enormous pile of pillows and cushions.

"Slip Sharpe's sweater over your T-shirt."

Her look was priceless with her eyes glowing in amusement.

His own expression had to be just about as funny. He definitely must be gaping in shock.

"You've got to be kidding me. Can't I just hold it in my hand?"

"You could, but we want Dandy to associate the scent with a whole, breathing human being, and we can best do that by you wearing the sweater."

"Next time let me bring one of my own old T-shirts," he said. "I like my own aftershave better."

"I'm going to take Dandy outside and give him a couple of minutes to run around. I need you to take a nosedive into that pillow fort over there and cover yourself up as best you can, okay? I don't want him to be able to see you at all. And try really hard not to move, either."

"On it," he said with a grin, jogging toward the pillow fort.

As soon as Felicity exited the room with Dandy, Stone dug himself into the bottom of the pile of cushions and pillows. Being six foot two and bulky with muscles, he was much too big to hide inside a pillow fort, even as large as he'd made it, with every pillow and cushion he could find in the room. He curled up as much as he could, wrapping his arms around his knees. It was hot under the cushions. He could barely breathe.

Though he felt like squirming, Stone continued to curl into himself, ignoring his cramping muscles, especially when he heard Felicity return with the dog.

Even so, it only took Dandy a matter of moments to find Stone. Dandy scratched at the pillows as if he was digging and barked with joy as he uncovered his new best friend, pouncing on Stone and licking his face with wild abandon.

"I don't even think you need Sharpe's sweater for Dandy to find you. That dog loves you so much he was completely homed in on you from the second we entered the room." She looked at her watch. "I think we should call it a day. You and Dandy have come such a long way together. Just look at all you've already done. Tomorrow we'll do some outdoor work around the center, so we'll be ready for the official avalanche training taking place next weekend in Bailey. I'll be doing my final certification and will be able to work with real teams after that. You'll be covering your initial certification."

"I'm so stoked for that."

Sadness briefly crossed Felicity's expression before she reined in her emotions and offered a shaky smile. "Yeah. Me, too. The more qualified teams we have, the more people we can save."

He felt he was being a little insensitive. She probably wasn't excited about becoming certified. She had a whole other set of reasons behind what she did. Yes, she was the one who'd brought up the subject, but that didn't mean it was easy for her to deal with. He greatly admired her willingness to face her fears.

He reached for her hand. "I'm sorry. I didn't mean—"

"Stop," she said, interrupting him. "I want you to talk about it, I want you to be excited about the opportunity to work with Dandy as a team and I don't want you walking on eggshells around me. You should be stoked about volunteering for the avalanche team. There have been more deadly avalanches in Colorado this year than ever before. They need teams like you and Dandy on their side to save lives."

"And you and Tugger," he added.

"Yes. And Tugger and me," she agreed, doing her very best to smile. "Now for your biggest surprise of the day."

"Really?" Stone brightened. "Bring it on. I love surprises."

Felicity chuckled. "Good to know. What would you think about bringing Dandy home with you tonight?"

"What? Really?" He'd never had a dog before, not even when he was young and had begged for a canine companion. His mom had been a single mother who had worked two and sometimes three jobs at a time to make ends meet and make sure Stone had everything he desired as a young adult. Without her, Stone wouldn't have been able to participate in high school rodeo or join the pros.

But because Mama was never around, she'd felt it wouldn't be fair to own a dog who would be left alone all the time.

But now—Dandy?

He already loved the dog. He and Dandy had definitely bonded over all the work they'd been doing together.

"So, what do you think?" she asked.

Stone put a sudden brake on his thoughts. "Are we talking about overnight tonight or from here on out?" he asked as it occurred to him that he might be jumping ahead of the game. It wouldn't be the first time. His breath caught in his throat as he waited for her answer.

"Oh." Felicity paused, her blond brow lowering. "I meant to give Dandy to you, since you'll be working as a team from here on out, but I definitely didn't think this all the way through. You're living with your mom right now. I'm not sure how she'd feel about having a high-energy dog around the house."

Stone gave it a few moments' thought before answering. "I honestly think Dandy would lift her spirits. He's a therapy dog as well as doing search and rescue, right? I have a feeling he'll know just how to win over Mama's heart. And he'll totally be my responsibility. I promise I'll take good care of him." He knew he sounded like a kid in a pet store, but he couldn't help his enthusiasm.

"I know you will. He's yours, then."

He definitely felt like a six-year-old boy finally getting the dog of his dreams. And for some reason, he also felt as if it was bringing him closer to Felicity.

Felicity laughed at his obvious eagerness. "And every moment you two spend together will strengthen your bond even more. Practice basic commands several times a day. Hang out in front of the TV together in the evenings. And be sure to place his bed right next to yours."

"Woo-hoo!" Stone pumped a fist. He couldn't help it. He just had to cheer.

"I like your enthusiasm. Let's get you set up with some food and training and grooming gear, then."

He grinned. He was feeling enthusiastic, all right. But now was probably not the right time to tell Felicity he was just as excited about working with her as he was with Dandy.

That knowledge, those feelings for Felicity, he would need to keep tucked away in his own heart for now.

Maybe for always.

Felicity was grateful to all her sisters for taking turns covering the gift shop so she could prepare Stone and Dandy for the avalanche rescue training. However, it did come at a cost. Even though she rarely spoke of it, Molly, Avery and Ruby were all very aware of her past with Trevor and the heartache she'd gone through, and they knew just how real her fear of avalanches was.

But that didn't stop them from teasing her about her relationship with Stone.

All of them remembered her goofy teenage crush on him and couldn't help rubbing it in now. It was embarrassing when they brought up the way she'd acted back then, but Felicity couldn't exactly deny it. She had been a typical angst-ridden teenager with her head in the clouds, melting like butter any time Stone was near.

As for her feelings for Stone now, she couldn't figure them out even within her own heart, much less be able to talk about them to others. What a muddled mess. She definitely didn't need her well-meaning but nosy sisters playing matchmakers.

Today, when Stone drove up to the A New Leash on Love facility parking lot, Felicity was already outside and, as usual, thoroughly bundled up for the weather. As she waited, she ran Tugger through various agility obstacles, more so Felicity could jog around and warm herself up than to relieve Tugger of his puppy energy. She took him up and down the A-frame and through a tunnel and then over a series of jumps, one after the other.

Stone hopped out of his truck and encouraged Dandy to do the same. As usual, Stone was only dressed in jeans and a long-sleeved Western shirt, winter hiking boots and a cowboy hat. She had given up trying to convince him he was going to freeze to death without a coat. Evidently his muscles worked like a jacket would because he certainly never complained about the cold, even when she felt it was freezing outside.

His grin was welcoming, and Felicity couldn't help but smile back at him, her heart welling. No matter how confused her emotions were, there was no doubt Stone was an exceptionally handsome man, just as he always had been.

"That looks fun," Stone said, gesturing toward the agility course. "Do all the dogs know how to do that?"

"It is fun," she agreed. "And yes, Dandy knows his way around the course. Maybe if you and Dandy still have some energy left at the end of the day you can try it out. But we have other fun things to do today first."

"Fun is always good in my book, as you well know. What's up first?" He reached down and scratched Dandy's ears.

The dog was heeling at Stone's left side without so much as a command, which thrilled Felicity to see. She didn't think Stone realized how far they'd come in such a short time and just what a great team he and Dandy made.

"We're going to play hide-and-seek."

"Awesome. I'm just warning you, though. You will lose. I am a master at hide-and-seek."

Felicity laughed. "The hiding part or the seeking part?"

"Both. Isn't that usually how it's played? You take turns hiding and seeking?"

"Usually," she agreed. "But not today. You and Dandy will be doing all of the seeking."

"And you'll be the one hiding?" he asked, raising his eyebrows.

Heat flooded her cheeks at the way his gaze shimmered at her with amusement and—something else she couldn't quite identify. "Yep. That would be me."

"I can work with that."

He winked, causing a blush to rise to her cheeks again.

"Don't you mean *we*?" she teased. "Remember, Dandy is the other part of your team. He may even be the better part as far as seeking is concerned."

"You're part of the team, too," he insisted. "You're my coach, and when we go to the official avalanche rescue training next week, you and Tugger are going to be my teammates, right?"

"When you put it that way, then yes. We're all a team." She couldn't have said why thinking about Stone as her teammate sent a kaleidoscope of butterflies loose in her stomach, but that was exactly what happened.

She struggled to clear her head, at length breaking eye contact with Stone so she could catch a breath.

"I'm going to run into those woods over there and hide," she told Stone, pointing toward the tree line. "Give me five minutes and then come find me."

"Five minutes? Why so long? I usually only count to ten."

"You've got to give me time to cover my

tracks. Otherwise, you'll just follow my foot-prints in, and that's no fun."

"I won't do that. I promise. Even if I catch sight of your footprints. After all, the point is for Dandy to find you, right?"

"Exactly." She unwrapped her red cro-cheted scarf from around her neck and handed it to him.

He lifted it to his nose.

She chuckled. "That's actually for Dandy to smell so he can catch my scent."

"Your perfume," he said. "The soft scent of roses. I'd recognize it anywhere. This is going to be way too easy for Dandy. I'd be able to follow your scent myself." He sniffed into the air and then barked, his tongue comi-cally lolling to one side, something he'd done more than once since she'd known him. She was beginning to think of it as his goofy puppy look, and it always made her heart turn over.

Felicity laughed so hard she doubled over with mirth. She couldn't remember ever laughing as hard as she did when she was with Stone. He brought such joy into her life every day.

"Should I hide my eyes in the crook of my

elbow against the tree and start counting?" he asked.

"You could, but that would be a long five minutes. Actually, why don't you take Dandy and go play on the agility equipment?" she suggested. "Time will fly much faster that way, and Dandy won't be able to watch which direction I go in."

When Felicity was certain Stone and Dandy were otherwise engaged, she jogged off into the trees.

The first thing she did was look for a long pine branch with lots of needles still attached to it. Once she found one that would work, she started dragging it behind her over the soft snow, erasing her footprints as she walked.

Farther in, she walked backward for a bit, not covering these tracks, making it look as if she was going one direction when she was actually going the opposite. It probably wouldn't throw Dandy off her tracks, but it might work with Stone, at least briefly.

She then started covering her tracks again as she hurried toward the hiding place she'd already selected. She knew exactly where she was going. There was a spot where some old pine tree roots had grown above the earth and wrapped around each other. It was the perfect spot to conceal herself, and one she'd often used as a child when playing hide-and-seek with her brothers and sisters.

When she reached the large copse of trees for which she'd been searching, she threaded herself into the winding roots, cocooning herself and making her body as small as possible, curling her legs up against her chest. Then she settled in for a long wait. Even with Dandy's help, she knew her hiding place was clever and hard to find.

She didn't remember it being so hard sitting in one spot without moving back when she'd been a kid, but perhaps she hadn't worried so much about not wiggling around in those days. As a child she'd always been busy, and it had been difficult for her to sit still. It had almost been more fun to be found than to hide.

She thought that might be the case even now.

It was getting cold. The wind was bitter, blowing snow from the trees and biting her cheeks, which were uncovered since she'd given her scarf to Stone.

All of a sudden, a large ball of wet snow showered over her. Whether she was supposed to be hiding or not, she stood abruptly and squealed loudly in surprise.

She whirled around to find a laughing and very-guilty-looking Stone, his light blue eyes sparkling with mischief and a light dusting of snow in his red-gold hair.

"How did you do that?" she asked. "Creep up on me, I mean. I didn't even hear you coming."

"Did I mention I'm sneaky?" His grin matched his words.

"Yes—but Dandy? He is supposed to alert by barking and I didn't hear a sound." She'd expected Dandy to find her first, and so she'd been listening for the dog, not the man.

"We worked together to find you. I was watching him carefully and knew we were getting close, so I put him in a down/stay and finished the search myself." He whistled and Dandy immediately came running to his side, which pleased Felicity to see.

"Is that so? And then when you found me, you just couldn't help yourself? You felt inclined to cover me with a gigantic snowball?"

she demanded. She propped her mittened fists onto her hips and tilted her chin saucily.

"Well, when the opportunity presented itself...how could I not?"

"Oh, you!" She reached down and scooped snow into her hand, quickly patting it into a ball before flinging it in Stone's direction.

To her delight, she beaned his ear with her throw, but moments later she realized that with her attack she'd just opened herself to counter retaliation.

A good, old-fashioned snowball fight.

Stone whooped and grabbed for some snow as Felicity did the same. Dandy didn't know whose side to be on, so he was a black blur running back and forth between them, barking merrily at whoever was in front of him.

Felicity got hit more than once, but she gave as good as she got—at least until Stone feinted scooping up a snowball and then ran toward her, snorting like a bull as he went.

He grabbed her around the waist and twirled her around several times before unceremoniously dumping her in a soft snowbank, laughing all the while.

Any victory he might have felt was short-lived, as she grabbed his shirt and yanked him into the snowbank beside her.

Chapter Ten

Stone had never had as much fun in his life as he was having working with Felicity and Tugger, and training every day with Dandy. Riding bareback in pro rodeo had given him consistent shots of adrenaline that he'd once craved and chased, but working with Felicity was a new adventure every day in a totally different way.

And every day he grew closer to Felicity, learning new things about her personality, what she liked and what she didn't, and he was quickly discovering she was as beautiful on the inside as the outside. He admired her intelligence and her sense of humor and the way she delighted in most everything she encountered.

He knew she'd been through a lot, and he

felt her struggles, especially with her faith. For a man who'd once been oblivious to other people's emotions, he was learning sympathy and empathy from Felicity, things he knew would serve him well in the future when he moved on to the rodeo school in Wyoming.

The thought of leaving Whispering Pines appealed to him less and less these days. Maybe it was that he was all-in on this avalanche dog training, but in some ways, he wondered what would happen if he put rodeo behind him for good. With his mother still dealing with her cancer treatments, it wasn't a decision he needed to make right away, but it was often on his mind.

Today, he and Felicity were digging several holes in the snow, everywhere from five to thirty inches deep, in which to hide a few of Felicity's rose-scented scarves. That Tugger and Dandy were able to smell scents at those depths amazed him, but Felicity assured him they'd been trained specifically to the scent of her rose perfume.

He definitely couldn't fault the dogs for being all-in on following *that* particular scent. It was quickly becoming Stone's favorite smell, as well. His heart always beat a little bit faster whenever he got a whiff of the light floral bouquet when Felicity was near.

"All done," he said, leaning back on his heels as he closed up the last and deepest of the six holes.

"Awesome. Now we can go back to the starting line and let the dogs do their thing. We'll follow right behind them."

They returned to where they'd left the dogs and released them from their down/stays. Both Dandy and Tugger were dressed in their bright red avalanche service dog vests that contrasted vibrantly against the white snow. Stone found it interesting how both dogs, even with their puppy energy, knew it was time to work when their vests went on.

"Let's let Tugger uncover the first one," she suggested as they approached the first scarf, which was buried five inches down. "Tugger, *find*."

The spotted brown pit bull sniffed the ground, his nose unerringly leading him straight to the correct spot, where he alerted with joyous barking while at the same time voraciously digging in the snow.

Felicity joined in, exclaiming excitedly.

Praising Tugger, she dug alongside the dog with her half-sized foldable shovel.

"Can't he dig the scarf out himself?" Stone asked, chuckling at Felicity's enthusiasm. "It's only a few inches down."

"Can he dig at five inches? Sure. Maybe even at a yard. But avalanche victims may be buried much deeper, so we always dig alongside our dogs. That way they're always reminded we're a team."

When she and Tugger reached the scarf, she let Tugger do the honors of rescuing it. He pranced around holding his head high, wagging the maroon-colored scarf in his jaws, clearly proud of his feat.

"Ready for your turn?" Felicity asked, grinning at Stone.

Stone and Dandy mirrored what Felicity and Tugger had just done, and within minutes Dandy had discovered a dark green scarf buried ten inches down.

They went back and forth with the dogs until they had retrieved the final scarf, which was teal-colored crochet. Even though Stone had watched the dogs do many remarkable things under Felicity's guidance since he'd first come here, it still blew his mind that the dogs could find something buried so deeply underground.

Their use in rescuing someone trapped by an avalanche must often make the difference between finding a victim alive or not, although Stone didn't say that aloud to Felicity, not wanting to accidentally trigger her or get her thinking about her past. He already thought he occasionally glimpsed grief flash across her gaze, and reflected once again on how amazing she was, facing down her fears for the sake of others.

"Great job with the scarves. Next up, Sharpe has hardpacked a snow fort for us to use over by the barn," Felicity told him.

They walked in companionable silence all the way back to the barn. Stone mused over the fact that they didn't always need to fill the space between them with endless chatter. He felt honored knowing it took a special kind of relationship to enjoy such a friendship.

The fort was good-sized and sandwiched between a couple of large lodgepole pines. A nearby aspen tree held an old tire swing that had been there since the time the Winslow siblings had been little, and was now used occasionally by Felicity's nieces and nephews.

"I'm going to take both dogs on a walk around the outside of the house and back over here. While I'm gone, hide behind the fort wall and pack a little loose snow around the edges so the dogs can dig you out and win the game."

"Got it," he said, his mind already spinning with a crazy plan that was sure to get Felicity laughing.

"Don't forget to bring the dogs into high drive when they figure out where you are. Praise them as if they just won a competition and be sure to play around with them when they find you. You're their prey, and to them it's a game," she reminded him.

"Yep," he called, and then turned to put the finishing touches on his masterpiece. This was going to be a blast.

Sharpe had done a wonderful job packing the snow fort with his Bobcat tractor. He'd raised it a good four and a half feet high, which was plenty tall for even a man of Stone's height to crouch behind, and three feet thick, to make it extra difficult for the dogs.

Felicity hoped Stone would have had enough

time to build up a ledge of soft new snow so the dogs would have something to dig through to find him. She expected Dandy to take a flying leap into Stone's lap. Man and dog had become incredibly close in the time they'd been working together. The fort itself would withstand their paws. It was rock-hard—Sharpe had packed it down with the tractor so it would be safe for the kids to play in it afterward.

When she returned to the fort with the dogs in tow, she immediately noticed a few changes, but not the ones she'd expected or directed. Stone had built up the wall as she'd instructed, but for some reason he'd added onto one side, slanting the wall to the ground at an angle. Maybe it was to give the dogs a little extra snow in which to dig, rather than having them climb over the top?

Dandy barked, alerting that he'd already discovered something. Probably Stone's aftershave, which Felicity especially liked. She released the Lab from his lead and let him run to dig out Stone, although it was more of an excited bolt through the air and into Stone's waiting arms, just as she'd expected it would be. The dog hadn't paid the least bit of attention to any of the extra snow Stone had packed in. He just bounded over it.

Now he was rolling around on the ground with his favorite person, barking and wagging his tail, licking Stone's chin and just happy to have found him.

"Woo-hoo. Way to go, Dandy!" Stone rolled to his feet and scratched Dandy's neck vigorously. "Who is my good boy?"

"Way to go, both of you," Felicity encouraged. "You and Dandy really do make a wonderful team together."

"Yeah?" Grinning, Stone jumped onto the tire swing and stood on it as he pulled himself back and forth.

"Careful, there. That swing wasn't made for full-sized cowboys."

"I'd better get off it, then," he agreed cheerfully before performing what she could only categorize as an uncoordinated swan dive. Hollering at the top of his lungs, he belly flopped onto the ledge of the fort, where he flipped over and landed on his back on the ground, hitting the trunk of the tree as he fell and causing snow from the branches above to dump on top of him, covering his entire body and most especially his face.

"Stone!" she called in alarm, her heart racing as she threw herself over the edge of the fort. Stone was completely covered except for his boots, and though he was struggling to sit up he was unable to move.

"Dandy, Tugger, *find*!" she commanded, using her own hands to scoop the snow away from where she believed his face must be. The dogs joined her and with their help she soon had an outline of Stone's body and knew better where to dig.

After a couple of minutes, Stone was sputtering and gasping and wiping snow out of his eyes. Felicity kept scooping around his shoulders and arms until he could sit up and brush the rest of the snow from his jeans on his own.

"Wow," Stone said, shaking his head and running a hand down his face as he stood to his feet. "Now, that was an epic fail if I've ever seen one."

"You just gave me a heart attack back there," Felicity snapped, glaring at him. "What in the world were you trying to do?"

He snorted. "Not that, obviously."

She narrowed her gaze on him even more and leaned back on her heels, crossing her arms. She tapped her foot as she waited for his real explanation.

"In my head, the way it was supposed to go off was that I'd jump from the tire swing to the fort's edge and then skid down the slide I made as if I was skateboarding or something. See?" He pointed at the diagonal he'd made against the fort, which Felicity had to admit did rather look like a slide now that she was observing it closer. "I wanted to try it out first to make sure the slide held. I thought the kids would like my addition."

"After what I just saw, I'm not so sure we should leave this fort up at all. You've just proven it's a major hazard."

She shivered with anger. She knew it wasn't Stone's fault. It was simply a prank that had gone wrong. More than likely, Stone would have been able to easily dig himself out of the snowdrift no worse for the wear except for maybe that moment when the snow had smashed into his face, and he'd had to struggle to find his breath. If he'd experienced a moment of panic, that was all on him.

Even though the rational side of her knew she couldn't blame him for the stunt gone wrong, the emotional side of her wanted to scream at him, to make him promise he would no longer take risks like that, that for once in his life he would think before he acted.

But if she did that, she would be admitting she was beginning to develop feelings for the cowboy—something that went beyond them working together on Winterfest, the gift shop and the training for avalanche rescue work.

She would be asking him to change his character, who he was as a man and how he approached life with the vigor that made him the person he was.

She wouldn't change who he was for all the world. But she also couldn't allow herself to be attracted to such a man. As with Trevor, Stone's recklessness would continue to nip at his heels—and hers, if she let it.

Hadn't he just proven that today? And that was to say nothing of the irresponsible motorcycle accident that had landed him in the hospital for over a month.

"What are you thinking about?" Stone asked. "You were far away there for a while."

She shook her head. "It's nothing."

"Hey," he said, reaching for her hand. "It's

not nothing. I know I frightened you back there, and I'm really sorry for that. But surely you can see it was an accident. There's no way I could duplicate that stunt if I tried. It won't happen again."

"How do you know that?" she snapped, yanking her hand from his grip. "You don't know. Nobody knows what's going to happen from one moment to the next—except maybe God. You could be walking down a road and have a tree fall on you. More than likely, you'll have been trying to swing from that tree." She blew out a frustrated breath and looked away from him.

Stone's brow lowered and he pressed his lips together. After a long pause, he shook his head.

"I don't know what to say. I've only just started reading the Holy Scriptures and applying them to my life. I wouldn't even be this far along if it weren't for the sacrifice of the hospital chaplain who visited me every day I was in a hospital bed. He never got tired of answering my questions, and believe me, I had plenty."

"I'm happy for you."

And she was. She really was. For most of

her life she'd been buoyed up by her faith. Her relationship with the Lord was what had kept her going through the hard times, up until Trevor's death. But now, when she needed it most, her spiritual life raft had apparently sunk.

"Maybe we could go talk to the pastor," he gently suggested.

She immediately shook her head. It was bad enough that she'd brought Stone into the dark night of her soul. She was miserable, and it was humiliating. And she didn't want to talk to a pastor or a chaplain who thought they had all the answers.

They'd see her through in a second as the fraud she was.

"Okay," he said, holding up his hands palm out. "Let's not go there. It was only a suggestion."

"I know. I appreciate it."

Actually, she just wanted to be done with this conversation.

"Tell me if I'm pushing too hard, but—"

"You're pushing too hard."

He sighed, but he didn't stop talking. "I know when I started having to deal with Mama's cancer diagnosis, I spent a lot of time reading the Psalms. I immersed myself in them. King David had some really dark times, too."

She hadn't picked up a Bible in months, but she recalled reading about King David's struggles and the poetic ways he'd called out to God for help when he most needed it.

Maybe it was time for her to do the same.

Chapter Eleven

Stone felt horrible for the way things had turned out the day he and Felicity had worked at the fort together. It had been a silly, lugheaded move to make, jumping from the tire swing onto the fort's ledge and trying to skid down the slide to the ground.

And all to impress Felicity, like a peacock displaying his feathers.

Only instead of impressing her, he'd frightened her half out of her mind, taking a literal nosedive into the snowy ground.

And it hadn't been the first time he'd done something like that with Felicity, either. It appeared to be a pattern with him. The harder he tried, the further he fell.

Yet even through all that, their friendship had blossomed. He hoped she knew how much he valued their time together. Despite the ways he kept dusting up trouble, there wasn't a person he more wanted to spend time with.

For days, he'd mused over what he could do to make it up to her for his big blunder, but he'd come up blank. Ultimately, he'd decided it was time to rope one of her sisters into it to try to help him out. They knew her better than anyone, after all.

After careful thought, he'd landed on visiting Avery. She'd shown how practical she was when she'd opened her bed-and-breakfast. He hoped she'd have some good ideas regarding something special he could do for Felicity.

He felt fine about it up until the point he was standing on the B and B's porch getting ready to knock on the door. Then suddenly he found himself wondering if what he was doing was a good idea or not. Was he inadvertently drawing attention to himself and Felicity? That was one thing he definitely didn't want to do.

He might have made a run for it had Avery not opened the door at that moment—before he'd even so much as knocked to make his presence known. She must have been watching for him. He swallowed his nerves.

"Come on in, Stone," she said, stepping back to allow him through the door. She was seven months pregnant with her third child and Stone could see the happy glow on her face. Of all the Winslow sisters, Felicity looked most like Avery, with their shared blond hair and blue eyes.

"How are you doing?" he asked with a grin.

She chuckled and pressed her palm to the left side of her rib cage. "Pretty sure this little one is going to be an NFL field goal kicker. Her punt is really sharp considering what little room she has in here."

"And are you feeling well?" He stumbled through the question.

"Oh, you mean like morning sickness?"

He actually didn't have a single clue what specifically he was asking, since the only things he knew about pregnancy were what he'd seen on television, and who knew how accurate any of that was?

"I had all-day sickness for the first four months and was *so* sensitive to smell. I was absolutely miserable, feeling nauseated all the time. I couldn't even be around food, much less eat it, which is kind of difficult when you're running a bed-and-breakfast. Jake helped a ton during that time. He really stepped up. Now, thankfully, I'm just feeling uncomfortably large." She threw back her head and laughed. "Everything you never wanted to know about pregnancy. Come on into the kitchen and pull up a chair and tell me what's on your mind."

"I appreciate you taking time out of your busy day for me." He held out a chair for Avery before seating himself across from her.

"Oh my. Felicity has caught herself a real gentleman."

Stone didn't even know how to respond to that statement, so he didn't, other than the way his face heated under her scrutiny.

"Jake took the kids to the park and our guests are all out training with Ruby at A New Leash on Love right now, so it's just the two of us. Feel free to speak up. I don't mind taking time for you at all. We're all here for you if you need us, you know."

Stone blew out a steadying breath and laid his hands flat on the tabletop. "Okay, so here's what happened." He told Avery the whole story of flipping off the roof of the gift shop and his epic fail with the fort, not leaving out any details no matter how humiliating they felt at the moment. She couldn't help him unless she knew the whole truth of where things stood between him and Felicity.

"Oh my," Avery said on a sigh, clapping a hand over her mouth. "You really did flip her switch, didn't you?"

He lowered his brow but nodded in agreement. "Epic. Fail. I know I triggered her when I pulled the stupid stunt, even though that was the last thing I wanted to do."

"She's told you about Trevor, then." It wasn't a question.

He nodded and leaned forward, clasping his hands in front of him. "So here's the thing. We've been working nonstop on avalanche training, and I know how hard that's been for her, even without my mucking around. I'd like to do something nice for her by way of apology for goofing around and not taking her seriously when I should have."

Avery's eyes lit up, but Stone couldn't tell what she was thinking.

"So you want to do something for her—or with her? What do you have in mind?"

"That's my problem. I've been thinking on this for a while now and am pulling a total blank. I feel like I know Felicity fairly well, but I can't think of anything that would truly make her smile."

"Hmm." Avery tapped her fingers against the table. It was a thoughtful gesture rather than a nervous one, but it made *Stone* nervous, particularly with the way she was looking at him, as if he were a specimen under a microscope.

"I've got it. I know exactly what you both need. Leave it to me and my siblings," she said with a mischievous smile that made Stone wonder if he'd done the right thing in coming to Avery for help.

"Okay," he said, drawing out the word.

"I'll let you know where you need to be and when you need to be there," she said. "Don't worry about a thing."

He hadn't been all that worried when he'd first asked Avery for help.

But now?

He wasn't so sure anymore.

"Do you trust me?" Stone asked, waving a blue bandanna under Felicity's nose. It was

Friday evening, and they were in the barn, where Stone had asked her to meet him after having worked the whole day in the gift shop together. She hadn't a clue why she was out here, and his suspicious behavior was making her curious about what his intentions might be. And now he was asking her if it would be okay to blindfold her?

Between his question and the gleam in his eyes, she was beginning to believe something out of the ordinary was happening.

Did she trust him?

"I don't know how to answer that." She eyed the bandanna doubtfully.

He laughed heartily. "Well, this isn't going to go very well for either of us if you're already balking, when we haven't even started yet."

"*What* isn't going to go well?" She switched her gaze from the bandanna to his twinkling eyes.

He sighed dramatically. "If I tell you what's going on, it won't be a surprise, now, will it?"

"A surprise?" Felicity parroted. She narrowed her gaze on him. In general, she was the type who liked surprises, but she was feeling iffy about this one. "Okay. But let me say up front I'm doing this under duress."

"Fair enough." He reached for her shoulders and turned her around, gently but firmly tying the bandanna over her eyes. "Can you see?"

"No."

"Good." He put one arm around her waist and grabbed her hand. "Don't worry. I won't let you trip or run into anything. I promise."

"Says the man who belly flopped into a snow fort."

"I thought we decided that was a one-off."

"Yes, but the brains behind that stunt aren't a one-off," she teased. "And that's what I'm worried about at the moment."

Quite literally completely in the dark, she clutched Stone's bicep. From the change in the temperature, she could tell he was leading her outside, but other than that, it was all she could do to concentrate on her footing and not trip.

He chuckled. "Then you'll be glad to know I wasn't the one who conceived this outing. I reached out to Avery for help, so if you want to blame anyone for what happens tonight, it's all on your siblings."

"My brothers and sisters?" She stiffened.

Knowing her siblings as she did, this wasn't exactly reassuring news. She'd been pranked by them—especially her brothers—more times than she could count over the years. And now Stone had just handed both of their lives to all of them on a silver platter.

Oh, what they could do with that.

"Okay, you can look now," Stone said.

Holding her breath, she pulled off the blindfold. They were standing behind the barn. The shires were right in front of them, harnessed up to the sleigh. Both the horses and the sleigh were beautifully decorated with silver and gold garland and tiny twinkling lights as well as the sleigh bells the horses usually wore during the Christmas season.

Felicity raised both hands to her lips. "Oh my," she breathed. "It's beautiful."

Stone grinned and held his hand out to her. "My lady. May I escort you to your ride?"

She accepted his hand and climbed up onto the sleigh. Stone jumped in after her and took the reins, expertly threading them through his fingers. She scooted close to him for warmth, laid the wool blanket he'd brought across both of their laps and curled her arm through his.

"Where are we going?" she asked, but he just flashed her a mysterious smile and didn't answer.

"Jack. Jill. Hup!"

The jet-black shires lurched forward as one. Felicity was impressed by how smooth their gaits were and how well matched they were, working together as a perfect team. They'd been fed well for weeks now, and their coats gleamed from frequent grooming.

And as for using a male-female team— Felicity couldn't find a single fault with Jack and Jill. Many guests had already complimented the Winslows on the drafts.

"You were right about the shires. They're a lovely pair. I'm happy you were there to pick them out."

He smiled down at her. "I'm glad you feel that way. I think so, too. Hopefully, your brothers are now starting to see their potential."

"I'm sure they are. Jack and Jill hardly look anything like the two shires we brought home from the auction. It's amazing what a little bit of tender loving kindness can do."

They rode in silence for a while, enjoying the February evening. It was unusually mild, and Felicity wasn't even sure she needed to be as bundled up as she was.

"So, where are you taking me, again?" she finally asked, not really expecting an answer, since he hadn't responded the first time.

"To be honest, I don't know much more than you do. I suspect your sisters were the ones who decorated the sleigh. They told me which of the three sleigh trails to take. I'm supposed to be on the lookout for—*something*. I guess I'll know it when I see it."

They most definitely knew it when they saw it.

They drove around a corner to the turn-around point, the large firepit where the guests were often taken for roasting marsh-mallows in the winter or hot dogs in the summer. There had been many singalongs with Frost playing his acoustic guitar. Stone knew it had been the scene of many a family pic-nic, as well.

The firepit was set with branches and kin-dling, and appeared ready to light, but the rest of the scene was entirely unique.

Rather than one of the picnic tables surrounding the circular area, a foldout table had been set with a white linen tablecloth and Felicity's mother's best fine china, which Avery had confiscated for the B and B just after it had opened. The dinner plates were covered as if it were a five-star hotel, and bottles of sparkling water stood next to sparkling crystal champagne glasses. She guessed even the silverware was, well, silver.

And it was romantic.

Her heart thundered. Was *this* Stone's idea?

"What's all this?" Felicity asked, glancing up at Stone and trying to read his expression for an answer.

"I don't—" His voice was especially husky, and he cleared his throat, his cheeks flaming red. "I really don't know. I was feeling bad about scaring you the way I did with that whole fort mix-up, so I asked Avery about it, and she reached out to your siblings for an idea about something nice I could do for you. I guess this is what they came up with."

Felicity felt embarrassed herself, but she chuckled at the way Stone fidgeted and pulled at the collar of the white T-shirt under his forest green Western shirt as if it were suddenly too tight and he couldn't breathe.

He wasn't the only one.

"Well, there you go, then. That explains it. Lesson number one—never ask my siblings to help you with anything. They'll use that as an excuse to stick their noses way up into your business. In this case, they are clearly matchmaking the two of us, whether that's what you asked for or not."

"I'm really sorry," he apologized with a deep, mortified groan. "I had no idea they'd misinterpret my intentions this way or I never would have asked."

Felicity swallowed hard, feeling as if he'd thunked her right in the heart. Of course he hadn't planned for this to happen or expected anything romantic out of the evening. Neither had she, so she didn't know why his words bothered her. But it still stung for him to brush it off this way.

In a way, she supposed it felt as if he were brushing *her* off.

"My brothers and sisters didn't misinterpret anything. You asked them to help, and they ran with it. No worries," she assured him.

"Well, we're here now. We may as well enjoy the food and the atmosphere, right?"

He hopped off the sleigh and offered his hand to her.

"And the company," she added, trying her best to smile even though her eyes were suddenly prickling with tears from emotions she couldn't identify, much less explain.

They approached the table, noting the calligraphed place cards. Her sisters had definitely gone above and beyond in every detail.

Next to Stone's plate was a note for them, written in what Felicity recognized as Ruby's handwriting.

"Interesting," Stone said, picking it up and holding it so they could both read the words at the same time.

"'Light the fire,'" Felicity read aloud, pointing to the can of lighter fluid and box of matches that had been placed on top of a cooler a few feet away. "I suppose that ought to be obvious. But look at the next one."

"'Flip on the portable generator and attach the plugs to the outlets next to the trees on the right side of the table,'" Stone read. "'Dessert is in the cooler. Enjoy your evening.'"

He swept off his hat and raised his eyebrows. "Do we dare?"

"I think we pretty much have to, or else

they may come barreling out of the trees screaming at us for ruining *their* evenings."

Stone stopped halfway through combing his fingers back through his hair, his face suddenly pale and his mouth agape.

"They aren't *watching* us, are they?" he rasped.

The expression on his face sent Felicity into a fit of giggles.

"They can certainly be brassy at times, but they wouldn't dare spy on us," she assured him. "Although my sisters, at least, will want a complete play-by-play when I get back this evening. Should I plug everything into the generator while you light the fire?"

Their eyes met and for a moment there was—*something*. Then Stone scrambled to grab the lighter fluid and the matches.

"Sounds like a plan," he muttered under his breath, and Felicity wondered what he was thinking.

Felicity found the portable generator and outlets just where she'd expected them to be, but she was surprised by the number of cords involved. As usual, her brother Frost had gone above and beyond. She plugged in one outlet and twinkling fairy lights appeared around the clearing, giving the area a soft, romantic glow. Another couple of plugs and music was streaming from speakers hidden somewhere within the tree line.

Not just music, but romantic music.

Every aspect of this scene screamed romance, and Felicity knew that wasn't by accident. She noticed the care her siblings had put into the meal, the decorations and the music, and she appreciated that they'd gone all out for her, showering her with their love.

They didn't realize their matchmaking was all in vain.

But how on earth was she going to be able to protect this assault on her heart?

Chapter Twelve

Stone's heart was beating a million times a minute as he squirted lighter fluid over the tepee-shaped branches and kindling, then tossed in a match to set it ablaze. The flickering of the flames mimicked his pulse, and he was in a certain state of panic.

He really hadn't known what to expect when they'd set off this evening, but a romantic dinner certainly wasn't it, and now he didn't know what to do.

He had thought dinner, maybe, but why not something more like what Winslow's Woodlands usually offered its guests? Why couldn't they sit at one of these picnic tables, enjoying barbecued beef on a bun, potato salad and baked beans eaten by the glow of the firelight. Maybe add Frost's acoustic guitar and rich baritone in the background.

Not that he wanted Frost here. Stone very much liked that it was just the two of them, but that was beside the point.

He half wanted to peek under the cover to see what the meal was, but he knew without even looking that they wouldn't be eating country barbecue here tonight. Not with everything else Felicity's siblings had put into this.

The twinkling fairy lights and the soft music gave the Winslow siblings away.

Matchmaking, indeed.

And the worst part was, he'd started all this. How was he supposed to work his way out of this now, especially since there was at least a small part of him that wanted to lean into tonight and see where the evening took them?

What he *didn't* want to do was somehow insult Felicity by saying or doing the wrong thing and making things worse than they already were. If she thought he'd suggested the matchmaking, he didn't want to tell her he didn't want any part of it, which would be outright rude and would definitely hurt her feelings.

On the other hand, he didn't want to push a romance between them when it was crystal clear that she was still struggling to process what had happened with Trevor.

He walked around to her side of the table and pulled out her chair for her in a grand, sweeping gesture. "What do you think?"

She eyed the chair for a moment before shrugging and offering a dramatic sigh.

"I suppose we may as well enjoy the meal, since they've gone to all the trouble of making it. And I have to admit I'm dying to know what Jake cooked us."

"How do you know it was Jake?" Stone asked curiously. Jake, Avery's husband, ran the bed-and-breakfast with her, so he supposed it made sense that Jake was involved, since Stone had gone to Avery first, and she had no doubt been inspired to create this scene in the first place.

"Oh, it's Jake, all right. No question. None of us kids really ever liked cooking, especially for as big a family as ours, and Jake does all the cooking for the B and B."

"You want to look at what we've got here?"

Stone was already holding on to the cover of his plate.

"Let's do this together," she suggested. "On the count of three. Ready? One. Two. Three!"

They simultaneously lifted off the covers to reveal thick ribeye steaks, loaded mashed potatoes and steaming asparagus.

Stone's stomach growled at the sight. "Now, *this* is a meal. I'm all in."

He reached across the table, his palm open before her, and asked, "Should we pray?"

He wasn't at all used to being in the position of suggesting a blessing over the food. Usually, he just prayed silently, or his mama would ask him to lead. But something—or Someone—prompted him to speak up.

Felicity met his gaze and stared deeply into his eyes for a moment without speaking. He swallowed hard, wondering if he should withdraw his hand, if he was pressuring her too much, but after a moment she put her hand into his, closed her eyes and bowed her head.

He followed suit, closing his eyes and bowing his head, as well.

"Father God," he started, but his throat

clogged with emotion, and he had to clear it before continuing.

Felicity squeezed his hand.

"Lord, we thank You for this time together. We appreciate You for everything You've done in our lives. Father, I pray You'll be with my mama and be gracious and merciful to her. Help her to feel Your presence always in her life and if it's Your will, Lord, heal her from her cancer and send her into remission. We trust in You for the best outcome."

He took a deep, ragged breath before continuing. "I'm grateful that You've put Felicity in my life and thank You for all she means to me. We ask that You bless us and this meal before us, through Christ our Lord. Amen."

"Amen," Felicity echoed softly. "And thank you, Stone, for the prayer."

"Sorry. I got kind of long-winded there." When Stone opened his eyes, he realized she had tears in hers.

"What's wrong?" he asked, wondering if somehow he'd made a mistake, or said or done the wrong thing. He knew she was struggling with her faith. Did she feel as if he was trying to force her to move forward with her relationship with God when she wasn't ready?

She shook her head, blinking and dabbing at her eyes with her thumbs in that way women did so as not to allow their mascara to smudge.

"Your prayer meant a lot to me. It really touched my heart. I pray for your mother every day, as well."

His own heart clenched at her words. "I'm glad. I meant what I said. I'm new to all this and I always feel as if I'm bumbling my way through my prayers. The chaplain at the hospital told me that I should just talk to God the same way I would a regular person, but..."

He paused, and she filled in the blank.

"God is so much more than that. He's in control. Thank you for reminding me of that."

He smiled at her and picked up his knife and fork. "Let's dig in."

To Felicity's surprise, conversation came easy as they ate, as they talked about everything from the work they were doing together in the gift shop and on avalanche rescue team training to his shifts driving the sleigh. They laughed over some of the guests who'd come through recently and the antics of some of the children they'd seen. They talked about their families, sharing stories from their pasts.

Stone gave Felicity an update on his mother. All the chemo treatments were wearing her down. She slept most of the time. He made sure she kept on top of taking her pain medications, though she rarely complained aloud.

"The worst part is I feel so helpless, like there's so little I can do for her," Stone said. "I know you've said before that my presence is important, but it just doesn't feel like enough, you know what I mean?"

"Yeah. It's a big burden for you to carry, especially when you're the type who wants to *do* something to make it better and you can't. I feel bad that I haven't come to visit her more often, but frankly, I've hesitated. I don't want to make things worse for her if she's not up to it," Felicity said. "I feel as if my being there might be too much for her."

Stone smiled, but she saw a glimmer of grief cross his gaze. He cut up a bite of steak and brought it to his lips, chewing and swallowing before speaking. "She'd probably enjoy a visit from you, as long as you keep it short. She's such a proud woman that she isn't going to tell you if it's too much for her even if it is."

"I'll make it a point to stop by, then, and I promise I won't stay long." She moved a stalk of asparagus around her plate but didn't eat it. Suddenly her stomach hurt, partly from thinking about poor Colleen and partly because of her next question.

"When are you planning on moving to Wyoming?"

He stared at his plate for a long moment. Without speaking, he put down his utensils.

"Honestly? I'm not sure. There's no way I'm leaving my mama until she's much better than she is right now. And even then..."

Felicity felt an immediate wave of relief that Stone was staying around for longer and then felt awful for experiencing it. She silently prayed for forgiveness for her selfish thoughts, though she knew Colleen would understand. She no doubt wanted Stone to remain in town as long as possible, as well.

"What do you think is in the cooler for dessert?" Stone asked, bringing Felicity back to the present.

"My guess? A couple of Ruby's husband

Aaron's famous cupcakes. He's really made a name for himself around here. Those are the yummy cupcakes we sell in the gift shop, and he supplies Sally's Pizza and Doug Little's ice cream parlor."

"He's the ex-marine, right?" Stone asked.

Felicity nodded. "A New Leash on Love has a substantial military contract thanks to Aaron. He came here to train with his new mobility assistance service dog and ended up marrying my sister. Go figure."

"That seems to happen a lot around here," Stone said with a laugh. "Men showing up in Whispering Pines and getting hooked into staying by a Winslow."

"I know, right? I'm the last unmarried sister." She felt a blush rising to her cheeks and hoped the setting sun covered it. "I'm fairly certain my brothers will be bachelors forever. They can be sweet when they want to be, of course, and I suppose they're handsome in their own way. They've never had a problem getting girlfriends, but I can't imagine a woman who could stand to live with either one of them on a more permanent basis."

Stone chuckled. "They may surprise you. One day they're certified bachelors and the next they've met the woman who will change their lives forever."

Stone caught Felicity's gaze, his eyes glimmering in the glow of the fire and the twinkling lights above them. Her breath slammed to a halt in her lungs.

"Let's look at the dessert," she blurted, scrambling to her feet and moving over to the cooler. She opened the lid fully expecting to see exactly what she'd told Stone they would have—Aaron's delicious cupcakes—but instead found nothing in the cooler except an odd-looking contraption and a couple of silicone oven mitts.

"What on earth is this?" she asked, holding up something that resembled a skillet except made with what looked like aluminum foil.

Stone moved to her side and read over her shoulder. "Popcorn?"

"Well, this is a surprise. How do we cook it? There's no microwave out here, and besides, wouldn't we blow the whole thing up with all the tin foil on this thing?"

"My guess is that we heat it over some charred wood in the firepit."

"Is this the way people made popcorn before microwaves?" Felicity asked.

"I've seen air poppers before, but nothing like this. This is going to be fun." He was grinning like a little boy on Christmas morning.

They were both laughing as Stone used a nearby stick to arrange some charred wood near the edge of the fire so they could pop their popcorn.

Felicity exclaimed in surprise and delight when the corn started popping, rising inside the covered skillet. "I feel as if we're in the olden days here."

"When do we take it off?" he asked. "We're gonna burn it, aren't we?"

"It's probably like microwave popcorn, don't you think? So we'll take it off the fire when it's only popping a kernel every few seconds?"

Felicity waited until she thought it was done, gave it a good shake and set it on a large nearby rock to cool down.

"Let me grab a steak knife off the table and see how we did." Stone plunged the knife into the top of the popcorn and steam poured out of it.

"Well, will you look at that," she said, admiring the perfect kernels of popcorn inside the foil.

"This is awesome," Stone agreed, carefully taking a few popped kernels in his fingers, blowing on them before shoving them into his mouth. "Yum. I feel as if we've been missing out on something super fun because we don't pop popcorn like this anymore. It's so much more exciting than just throwing a bag in the microwave and setting the timer."

Stone grabbed bottles of water from the table and the two of them settled on a large log next to the firepit to eat their popcorn and enjoy the warmth of the fire.

Ever since Felicity had turned on the generator, love ballads from the eighties, nineties and into the next century had been flowing out from the speakers hidden in the background, loud enough for them to hear the words but not so much as to be difficult to talk over. Cheesy, but Frost knew they were Felicity's favorites.

For the most part, Felicity hadn't even noticed much of the music except to think about how Frost must have taken quite some time out of his day to make such an epic playlist for her. If she wasn't mistaken, it had been running a long time without repeating songs.

And then it happened.

The song started playing—the one Felicity had most associated with Stone while growing up. That Frost had selected this particular song for their playlist was a coincidence weird enough to shake Felicity up, and she practically choked on her popcorn.

It was the one and only time Stone had ever paid her any attention back in middle school, and she'd tucked that memory away and held it close to her heart.

She'd been at a middle and high school dance. With Whispering Pines being such a small town, the school dances were always a mix of middle and high school students. She'd been out on the floor with her closest girlfriends, enjoying dancing around to the fast beat of the music when suddenly the DJ had announced a couples dance to the very song that was now playing from the speakers.

She'd been so shy as a teenager, and somehow at that moment she'd gotten separated from her friends. Couples were forming all around her, hemming her in on the dance floor. In hindsight, she should have simply made her way to the side with the other wallflowers, but for some reason embarrassment had overcome her and she'd just stood there frozen to the spot, feeling ridiculous but unable to move.

Suddenly, out of nowhere, Stone was there by her side.

"Hey, Felicity. Are you okay?" he'd asked her, concern in his gaze. She must have looked as panicked as she'd felt. "You don't look so well."

"I—I lost my friends," she'd babbled, thinking about how foolish that must have sounded. She remembered the heat that had risen flaming to her face. If she'd been embarrassed before, she was a hundred times more so now.

"I see Ruby over there," he'd told her, pointing out her sister to her.

Felicity was one hundred percent certain Ruby wouldn't want to be hanging out with her little sister in public. Ruby had a boyfriend as well as all her high school friends. In fact, Felicity was surprised Ruby wasn't currently out on the dance floor with her boyfriend.

But anything was better than foolishly standing as still as a statue in the middle of the floor, in the way of all those people who *did* have partners. She just wanted to cry, and then she felt silly because she could barely hold back tears.

Stone's gaze never left her. After a moment, he took her elbow and gently led her toward her sister. Felicity's knight in shining armor. Stone had never looked as good to her as he did at that moment.

"Yeah. Thanks for the help. Have a good one," Felicity had finally blurted out. Then she'd scurried off so quickly she hadn't even given Stone a chance to respond.

She smiled, remembering that awkward scene from her youth. Stone probably wouldn't even recall the encounter, though it had meant the world to her at the time.

"What?" Stone asked, bringing her back into the present. "What's that smile for? You've got to tell me."

"This is our song," she said with a laugh, happy beyond words that she was no longer that timid, awkward teenager and could actually hold a conversation with Stone Keller.

"*Our* song?" he asked, appearing confused.

Felicity proceeded to tell him the whole story of his gallant rescue—at least, from her perspective it had been. For him it had been nothing at all.

"Hmm," he said, shaking his head. "Sorry. I totally don't remember that. It doesn't sound at all like me, though."

"I know, right?" she teased, laughing at the expression on his face.

He scrubbed a hand down his jaw and chuckled. "I know I wasn't the most thoughtful guy back then. Kind of self-centered, really."

"I never noticed." And she really hadn't. Not back then. When she'd been in middle school and Stone was in high school, Stone could do no wrong in her eyes. He was the ideal of perfection, as far as she was concerned. And that night at the dance, when he'd saved her from herself, he'd been her knight in shining armor.

He stood in front of her and held out his hand.

She stared at it without moving. "What is this?"

"My hand," he said, raising his eyebrows as if it wasn't obvious.

"Yes, I know that, but—"

"Consider it an invitation. After that story you just told me, I think I owe you one."

"Owe me one? How do you figure?" she asked, thoroughly confused. She wasn't following at all. He'd done something nice for her, and somehow, he thought *he* owed *her*?

"Oh, come on, Felicity. I should have asked you to dance that night, not pushed you off to your sister. I'm rectifying that now."

Felicity's heart soared as her eyes met his.

"Don't leave me hanging here." His smile widened as she finally put her hand in his and he helped her to her feet.

"I'm not much of a dancer," she insisted. She had no idea why she was trying to talk herself out of this, the fulfillment of a long-held dream.

Perhaps because deep down she knew better. She'd left her teenage crush behind her long ago.

This—she didn't know what this was.

Stirring up something from the past, perhaps.

"Well," said Stone, his raspy voice deepening, "it just so happens that I'm an excellent dancer. All you have to do is put your arms on my shoulders and I'll do the rest."

She'd left reality the moment he'd offered his hand to her, and now she was certain she must be dreaming, floating on clouds as his large hands clasped her waist and she rested her palms on his shoulders.

He met her gaze and smiled down at her before pulling her close, gently swaying in the moonlight. Quietly, he hummed along with the song, his breath warm against her cheek. She laid her cheek against his chest and could hear the beating of his heart.

He leaned back so he could look into her eyes, his own sparkling in the light of the fire. Slowly, he smiled, and it lit up his whole face. Then his gaze dropped to her lips. He pulled her closer until she could feel his stubbled cheek against hers and they swayed slowly together.

Then his mouth touched hers. It felt completely new and unexpectedly authentic at the same time, as if they had been here before and would be again, communicating far more than either one of them could say with words.

"Felicity," he murmured in the low, raspy voice that always made her heart sing. He said her name once more before kissing her again.

And a dream, a long time in coming, finally came true.

Chapter Thirteen

It had been a week since Stone and Felicity's special dinner, and for Stone, their kiss had changed everything. He supposed he'd known for some time that his heart was being called home to Whispering Pines for good. His attachment to his hometown was growing stronger with the time he was spending with his mama and his deepening relationship with Felicity.

He was ready to show Felicity how much she meant to him. He just had to figure out how and when, and he thought his mother might be able to help with that. He'd always been able to talk to Mama and ask for her advice, though there were many times in his life when he hadn't been receptive to what she had to offer.

Now he was.

He'd made up a tray for her lunch. She still spent more days than not in bed with a fatigue so great she could barely lift a limb. But today she'd decided to rest in the recliner in the living room and watch television on their larger screen. He had set her up with extra pillows and blankets and made sure she had all the remotes she needed within reach.

Despite her ever-constant pain, her eyes lit up when Stone entered the room with the tray full of goodies. He'd even purchased a small bouquet of flowers at the local store when he'd picked up groceries for the meal. Hopeless as he'd been at cooking and cleaning when he first returned to Whispering Pines, he now did nearly all the cleaning, cooking and shopping. He still wasn't great in the kitchen and Mama had to deal with eating very basic meals, but because of her mouth sores she didn't care for much beyond what Stone was able to cook, anyway.

Today she was wearing a soft turquoise turban. Although she was now past chemo, her hair hadn't yet begun to regrow, and she was greatly anticipating getting it back again. Hopefully still red, she'd told Stone, because she was proud of her Irish heritage, but she would be fine with extra curls, as she'd heard sometimes happened when hair grew back after treatment.

Count on his mother to look at the bright side of things. As far as he was concerned, she was beautiful just as she was, even after the ravages of chemo.

"What's on your mind?" she asked him as he sat down on the sofa opposite her and propped his stocking feet on the coffee table in front of him.

He clasped his hands behind his neck and stretched, looking at the television instead of at Mama, because it always felt as if she could read his thoughts in his eyes.

"What makes you think I have something on your mind?" he asked with a chuckle.

She looked straight at him and huffed. "I brought you into this world and I raised you up right good. I can read you like a book, young man, and right now you look as if you're going to crawl out of your skin. So tell me what's bothering you, son."

He blew out a breath. "I'm not such a young man anymore."

"Stop stalling, kiddo, and spit it out."

"It's Felicity."

A knowing smile lit up her face. "Honestly, I would have been surprised if it wasn't. You've been spending quite a lot of time with her lately."

"I've been praying a lot about her, too," he admitted. "I could definitely use a woman's perspective about how Felicity might fit into my life. We've been getting close," he said, stuttering to a stop to avoid having to explain just how close they were.

"I think—no, scratch that. I *know* that she is my person. I just have to figure out how to let her know that's how I feel about her." The fact that he was afraid of how she might react to such a thing, he didn't say aloud.

Colleen's eyes twinkled as she chuckled. "There are tried and true methods, you know. A diamond ring. Going down on one knee."

"Isn't that cliché?" He scoffed and shook his head. "Besides, I don't know if I may be rushing things a bit. The last thing I want to do is give her the wrong kind of surprise and send her running off into the woods. After what happened with Trevor—well, I just want to make sure I'm not pushing her too fast."

"Trust me. Women like cliché when it comes to things like a proposal." She patted the arm of her chair. "But you're right about not pushing her. Come here, sweetheart."

Stone moved to his mother's side, putting his arm across the top of her chair and kissing her on the forehead.

"There's no reason to hurry," she advised him. "Wait until the moment feels right. You'll know when that is. Trust God to show you the way and He always will."

"I will." Stone's heart was lodged firmly in his throat at his mother's wise words. As always, he knew he could depend on her.

"Now," she continued. "For the ring."

She pulled the ring from her right hand and placed it into Stone's hand, closing his fingers over his palm.

"Your claddagh ring?" Stone tried to swallow but couldn't. "But Mama—"

"This ring has been in our family for generations, usually passed down from daughter to daughter. My grandmother gave it to my mother, and my mama gave it to me. But since I never had a daughter, I would love it if you gave it to Felicity."

He knew the basic story of Mama's claddagh ring. Inside were engraved the words:

Friendship. Loyalty. Love.

The ingredients of every great marriage, with faith in God as a given.

Tears pricked at Stone's eyes.

"A claddagh ring is especially perfect for your particular situation. It means different things depending on the way it's worn. It's way better than announcing your relationship status on social media." Their eyes met and they both broke into laughter.

"If you decide to give Felicity the ring as a promise ring to show her your love and commitment, place it on her right hand with the point of the heart facing the hand.

"When you propose, the ring will go on her left hand with the heart pointing out. The day of your wedding, you'll turn that heart inward to promise forever.

"I never had that kind of relationship with your father, but my parents did, and I wish the same with all my heart for you. Still, son, I don't want you to feel pressured to use this ring if you want to do something different.

She may prefer a more traditional solitaire. You have to take into account what Felicity would like best."

"Are you kidding? Family is everything to Felicity, and she of all people will appreciate the history behind this. It'll mean as much to her as it does to me. Mama, I can't thank you enough."

He took her hand and kissed her too-cold fingers, and she pressed her palm against his stubbled cheek, but her arm soon weakened, and she dropped it into her lap.

He eyed the ring gratefully and smiled down at his mother. She had given him everything he needed.

Now he only needed to figure out where and when to give it to Felicity.

Felicity had been working herself up to this moment for months, but it still took every ounce of her courage to be standing on the snow-covered mountain with this group of avalanche rescue trainees. This was her third and final certification, and would be Stone's first if he and Dandy passed today.

She wasn't sure she would have the strength to be here were it not for Stone's presence by her side. He had done so much for her, supporting her as she slowly regained her faith in God, giving her an extra boost of confidence when she needed his strength and—well, she didn't know if she could count the kiss or not. That had just happened, maybe as a result of the romantic atmosphere her siblings had created, or maybe because of the story she'd told him of the time he'd rescued her at the school dance.

But there would be time to work out the direction their relationship might be heading—or not—later. Right now she had to pay attention to what the trainers were saying about the day's events. This day was oh-so-important in so many ways.

"The rescue today is especially for the expert level training, though we've got a few initial certification teams here today. You and your dogs will be seeking and finding some of our trainers, who will be waiting for you in the specially dug-out graves."

Despite doing her best to remain calm, Felicity started to sweat as she crossed her arms. Stone put his arm around her.

"Are you going to be okay?" he asked softly.

"Couldn't they come up with a better term for the human-made dugouts than to call them graves?" she whispered with a ragged shudder. "Can't we just call them dugouts?"

Stone pulled her even closer.

"Before we start, I need everyone to sign your waivers and turn in your practice logs," the captain of the team announced.

"So this is why we had to dig out so many scarves," Stone said as he signed his name and indicated he was working with Dandy the Labrador retriever. "To prove we're ready to take on the real thing."

"Right. After we get our certificates, we may be called on to work with our dogs in a real avalanche emergency."

"And you're going to be okay with that?"

His concern was obvious, and she appreciated how much he cared, but she wished he wasn't always questioning her commitment to this program.

The way she saw it, Trevor was the reason she'd originally signed up for this program. Granted, Trevor had been snowboarding off-grid, so it was far less likely that an avalanche rescue team would have been near.

But if they had, they might have made all the difference between him living and dying.

Seeing people displaced from their homes because of avalanches like the one that had happened in Holden Springs only added to her determination, but at the end of the day, this was what she felt God was calling her to—search and rescue in Colorado's often snow-covered mountains.

When the time came for the real thing, she would be ready to head out and attempt to rescue the victims of an avalanche. Because that was the least she could do.

"Listen up," the captain shouted, and the trainees and their dogs all quickly gathered around.

"One of our lead trainers had a family emergency today and couldn't be here, so I need one of you all to step forward, preferably an initial trainee, and be willing to be buried in a grave. I promise it's not nearly as bad as it sounds. The dugouts are quite comfortable and surprisingly warm. They've been carefully created and are constantly monitored by drones. You can use your cell phone to catch up on your email and social media while you relax and wait to be found. Anyone?"

To Felicity's utter shock and surprise, Stone's hand shot into the air before anyone else could move. Her gut immediately started churning.

How could Stone put himself in this position, no matter how safe and well monitored the exercise would be? Didn't he know how much this would upset her?

She could think of many reasons for him *not* to do this. For one thing, he wouldn't have the opportunity to work with Dandy and therefore wouldn't receive his initial certification today. And maybe it was selfish on her part, but she'd been looking forward to working with Stone and Dandy today as they searched for their "victims."

But in typical Stone fashion, he'd leaped before he looked, raising his arm to volunteer before thinking it all the way through. She actually had no idea what he was thinking at all.

Maybe he'd assumed this would be exciting. But he was bound to be disappointed. He'd just volunteered to be bored all afternoon.

"Why'd you do that?" she whispered raggedly, trying to keep the annoyance she was feeling out of her tone, and wanting to grab him by the shoulders and shake him. He was crating Dandy, whom he would no longer be needing.

It completely floored her when he grinned back at her, almost looking excited at the prospect of hanging around in a cave. "No worries, right? Totally safe?"

"Well, yes, but that makes me question your motives even more. Sitting in a snow dugout for two hours while the dogs find you isn't exactly adrenaline-chasing behavior. You'd be far better off on the other side of the leash. And you aren't going to be the only one to suffer. Poor Dandy is going to miss all the fun, too."

She didn't add that she'd been looking forward to working with him when he clearly didn't feel the same way about her. Nor did she point out that he'd managed to botch the *totally safe* snow fort and had given her a real scare when he'd practically buried himself in the snow.

If he wanted to hang out in a grave, so be it. She and Tugger had a job to do. It might not be as fun to her as it was to other teams, but they would be receiving their final certification today, whether or not Stone was by her side.

Chapter Fourteen

Stone's pulse was pounding, and electricity was making every nerve snap with anticipation. Felicity thought his waiting in a monitored avalanche grave was going to be boring for him.

She had no idea just how *not* boring it was going to be.

His hand had shot up before his idea was even fully formed in his mind, but now that he was able to think all the way through it, he was even more excited than when he'd first conceived of his plan.

He pulled the captain aside and explained his intentions, getting the lead trainer on board for sending Felicity and Tugger in the right direction. Stone's idea would only work if Felicity and Tugger were the ones to find him.

He made himself as comfortable as possible in the dugout, leaning his back against the wall and stretching his legs straight out in front of him, crossing them at the ankles. It wasn't great, but it would have to do.

Now all he had to do was wait.

He reached into the pocket of his vest to grab his cell phone to check if there was service—not that it really mattered, as long as the camera function was working. He definitely wanted pictures of the special moment to share with family.

His fingers reached inside his vest pocket to touch the box that held the claddagh ring, which was about to change his life for better or for worse.

His mind and heart were in a constant state of prayer. Today meant everything.

Felicity meant everything.

Stone took the ring out of the box and held it between his fingers, admiring its sparkle. The inside of the heart was emerald green, while diamonds surrounded the heart and the crown above it. Because she owned his heart and to him, she was royalty.

He'd decided to make a solemn promise to her today that his heart was hers. He would place the ring on her right hand, heart pointed toward the hand, and would explain exactly what that meant to him.

Then, when the time was right, he would gather her family and his mom together and propose to Felicity, making official what he already knew in his heart to be true. Maybe he'd have her siblings set up another romantic evening like the last one they had.

But for this first time he wanted it to be just the two of them so he could explain the significance of the ring passed down by his mama.

Smiling broadly, he returned the ring to the box and tucked it back in the pocket of his vest. He picked up his cell phone, whistling to himself as he prepared to wait for as long as necessary for the big moment to come.

The dugout sheltered him from the bitter wind blowing outside, and soon he became warm and shed his vest, though he kept it close beside him.

He'd be a married man. Whoever would have thought that when he'd returned to

Whispering Pines, his best friend's younger sister would be the woman of his dreams?

He'd considered this a hundred times over. Maybe he was rushing things in his mind, but now that he'd made his decision and reconciled his feelings, he didn't want to wait any longer to start forever with Felicity.

He yawned and checked the time. Only forty-five minutes had passed. He wasn't sure when the actual search had started, so it could still be a while before Felicity and Tugger found him. He'd figured an hour and a half, at least.

But he wasn't any good at waiting. No wonder Felicity had been confused when he'd offered to man a dugout. This wasn't his thing at all.

Yawning for the second time, he decided a little nap was in order. It wasn't as if he was going to miss anything. He tipped his cowboy hat down over his eyes and crossed his arms over his chest.

In moments, he had drifted off.

He didn't know how much later it was when he was suddenly awakened by a sound he didn't immediately recognize.

At first, he thought it must be the rescue

team having caught scent of him, and he listened to see if he could distinguish Tugger's singular bark and Felicity's high-voiced encouragement over the sound of the wind whistling through the trees.

Anticipation built in his chest. It was almost time.

He grabbed his vest but didn't have time to put it on before the reverberation once again reached his ears.

It wasn't the sound of dogs barking or people shouting. Rather, it was a rumbling, at first soft, which became increasingly louder, hard enough to shake the ground at his feet and the walls around him.

He immediately knew what was happening.

An avalanche.

He almost couldn't believe it was real. Of all the things that could possibly be happening right now, a real avalanche when rescue teams were working on getting their certifications? How was that even possible?

Suddenly snow rushed down and covered the entrance to his dugout, a big whoosh of white powder that completely blocked the sun. He rushed over to the entrance and tried to push his hand out through the snow, but it was thicker than he'd imagined it to be, and he couldn't reach the outside.

He knew the dugouts were all constantly monitored by drones. The lead trainers had created the dugouts themselves and would know exactly where to look to find him if something bad happened. But if he was buried under the snow for any length of time, would it really matter if they had him on their GPS?

Would this practice grave turn into a real one?

Dropping to his knees at what had been the entrance to the dugout, he cupped his hands together, scooping away snow as quickly as he could, aware that with his work, his breathing was coming in quick bursts, taking up valuable oxygen. This might be a problem if he remained stuck in the dugout for any length of time.

Most of the snow that had fallen over the entryway was soft, but he quickly discovered that as he scooped, more snow fell over the entrance. It was useless to keep digging but he did it anyway.

Just then, the side of his wrist came down

hard on a sharp rock he hadn't even realized was there. Pain splintered through him as he tucked his wrist to his chest and sat back on his heels.

He gently tested the area around his wrist and closed his eyes in agony. The pain was excruciating. His wrist was definitely fractured—exactly what he didn't need right now. Without two good hands to help him, there was no way he could dig himself out, not that he could have done it on his own anyway.

He was now injured and completely buried. His only hope was that the dog teams would find him in time.

But what if they didn't? He knew Felicity and Tugger were in the lead toward his grave. After all, he'd asked the captain in charge to point her toward his dugout. But this wasn't anything at all like he'd hoped the day would go.

At this point, he became aware that the worst could very well happen.

Felicity could find him too late.

He was already on his knees, so he turned his mind to prayer. Oddly enough, he didn't feel any sense of panic that he might well be facing his own death. He'd already made his peace with the Lord, and he could rest with that peace in his heart.

His only fear was what his death would do to Felicity, not to mention leaving his mother on her own. He knew for Felicity, after losing Trevor, it was something she would have difficulty coming back from. He was also experiencing an anguished sense of sadness that he wouldn't have the opportunity to spend a long life with her.

But he gave that, too, up to the Lord.

His last prayer before he lay down and curled up around his vest, gently cupping his broken wrist in his good hand, was for Felicity, that she wouldn't lose her faith because of what happened to him, but rather that some good would somehow come out of it.

He tried to keep his breathing slow and even, to stretch out the rest of the remaining oxygen as much as possible.

Then he put himself in the Lord's hands and closed his eyes.

"Attention, all teams. Meet back at base camp immediately!" The team captain's voice sizzled through the walkie-talkie radio clipped to Felicity's belt.

"I wonder what that's all about?" she muttered to Tugger, who was completely focused on his job.

Several teams had already reported back on their transmitters that they had found their "victims" and were already headed back to headquarters.

Was Stone among them?

Felicity and Tugger had yet to find anyone, despite the captain giving her specific directions on which way to search. She wondered again if Stone had yet been found, or if he was still out there waiting in a dugout. In some ways she wanted to be the one to find him, but now she felt as if she might be heading in the wrong direction, since she and Tugger hadn't yet stumbled on a dugout.

She was about to turn back toward the base camp as the captain had insisted, when suddenly Tugger alerted and started barking frantically, straining on his lead for her to follow him. Her gut always told her to follow her dog, but she'd just had instructions to do otherwise.

"All teams, please return to base camp immediately," the captain repeated, his voice crackling through the radio. "We have an emergency."

An *emergency*?

Was this part of the trial certification, some kind of mock emergency? Or was this for real?

Stone.

Felicity's heart pounded so hard she could hear it in her ears. She didn't even realize she was praying aloud.

"Lord, keep Stone safe. And be with the victim involved in the emergency."

If there really was an emergency.

She did know there was a "victim" somewhere close at hand, because Tugger was still alerting desperately.

She pulled her walkie-talkie from her belt. "Captain, this is Felicity Winslow. Red Four," she corrected herself, using her call sign.

She waited without breathing for the captain to acknowledge her on the two-way radio.

"Go, Red Four."

"I know you just called all teams back and it's probably part of the trial for Tugger and me to return as well, but Tugger just alerted. I feel as if I'm really close to one of the graves. Should I continue searching or return?"

Her breath caught in her throat. She wasn't sure about all the procedures, but she was fairly certain she'd just broken rank.

"What are your GPS coordinates, Red Four?"

She checked her cell phone app and quickly rambled off the coordinates, eager to allow Tugger to take the lead and find their "victim."

Hopefully, she wouldn't be disqualified because she was questioning the captain's orders, but she had to try.

Finally, the captain's voice crackled through the radio.

"If Tugger is alerting, follow his lead. But be extremely cautious as you move forward as there may be more avalanche activities in the area. Our drone caught one avalanche, and although it was relatively minor, we believe it may have covered the entrance to Stone Keller's grave. So time is of the essence. You and Tugger are closest to him. This is not a drill. Repeat, this is *not* a drill. Our teams will be there to back you up as soon as possible."

The moment Felicity heard Stone's name, everything else faded into the background.

"Oh, Lord. Save him."

But in the same breath, she realized God would have to work through her to save Stone. Instead of weakness, she suddenly felt strength. Even as she was following Tugger's alert, prayers were pouring from her heart.

"I'm here, Lord, opening myself up to You. Guide me to Stone and help me to rescue him."

Abruptly, Tugger stopped straining forward and started voraciously pawing at a snowbank. His bark changed, and Felicity quickly examined the entire area. Tucked against the mountain, it was the perfect place for the lead team to have placed a dugout.

Her heart ached like no other, but this was absolutely not the time and place to examine the flood of emotions streaming through her.

"Stone?" she called as she dropped her backpack and grabbed her shovel, digging in the area next to Tugger, encouraging the dog to continue his work.

"Stone? Can you hear me?"

No answer.

The snow was deep, but it was mostly

soft powder from the minor avalanche. Felicity worked as fast as she could, calling out Stone's name again and again to no avail. With every second that passed, her heart beat faster and her breath came in shorter.

She heard the welcome sound of barking dogs just as she finally broke through the snow and into the dugout.

"Stone? Stone?"

She thought she heard a groan and redoubled her efforts to get inside, flinging the snow backward and widening the hole until it was big enough for her to crawl in.

Behind her, other teams appeared, and other dogs and their trainers immediately joined in clearing the entrance to the dugout.

Felicity was the first one in, scooting on all fours until she was next to Stone, who was curled up on the floor in the middle of the dugout. At first, he didn't look as if he were moving at all, maybe not even breathing, and panic seized her, making every nerve scream.

Relief washed over her when she saw Stone's chest rise and fall, though her anxiety was still snapping. Why wasn't he responding when she said his name?

He blinked his eyes and emitted a low groan. "Felicity?"

"Stone? Sweetheart? Do you know where you are?"

He gritted his teeth and tried to sit up, but Felicity gently pushed him back to the ground, scooting to his head and holding his neck steady. "Carefully roll onto your back and lie still." Her command was firm but soft. "We don't know how badly you've been injured. Don't move your head until an EMT can evaluate you."

"I'm okay," he insisted. "The only thing that hurts is my wrist. I think I busted it trying to dig myself out."

Only then did she notice the way he was hugging one hand to his chest with the other. "We'll get it checked out, sweetie, but let's not get ahead of ourselves here." Tears pricked her eyes, but she refused to let them fall. Gently, she steadied his head with her palms, stroking his temples with the pads of her thumbs.

The captain and two EMTs crawled into the dugout and assessed Stone's condition, placing a neck brace around him just in case of spinal injury and putting an oxygen mask over his mouth and nose.

He fought it, wanting to speak, but Felicity put her hand over his and shook her head. "You need the oxygen. Who knows how long you were deprived? We can talk later after they've had the opportunity to fully assess you."

The EMTs brought a toboggan into the dugout and carefully rolled a blanket under Stone and transferred him to the toboggan.

"We've got a helicopter waiting in the clearing by the base camp," the captain told her. "We'll get Stone there as quickly as possible, and I'll let you know how it goes."

If the captain thought he was taking Stone away without her, he had another think coming. There was no way she was going to leave Stone's side, at least not until he was taken away by the life flight.

"Let me harness Tugger to the toboggan," she pleaded. "He's an excellent puller and Stone trusts him."

The captain pressed his lips together as he considered her request, but after a moment he jerked a nod. "Okay. Harness him up."

Felicity harnessed Tugger to the front of the toboggan and gave the captain a thumbs-up.

"No," Stone wailed. He reached out his good hand and grabbed at the fabric of Felicity's snowsuit. "My vest. You've got to get my vest."

"Because of your cell phone?" she asked. She pulled it out of her own vest pocket. "I've got it right here, Stone. Now, try to take it easy."

He tried to shake his head, but it was impossible in the brace, and it made him groan again, but he grabbed at her, nonetheless.

"No. No. My vest. You've got to get my vest."

She couldn't imagine what was so important about his vest. Maybe he was in a state of shock because of lack of oxygen or his broken wrist, but he was clearly in a state of panic over his vest, so she returned to the dugout and grabbed the vest, tucking it under her shoulder and returning to Stone's side.

"I've got it. See? Try to relax," she told him. "Take deep breaths. We're going to get you out of here and get that wrist looked at, okay?"

He breathed out heavily and closed his eyes.

For Felicity, and no doubt for Stone, it felt as if it took forever to return to base camp, but at least she was by his side. He was being strong and stoic, but she could tell he was in pain, and she wondered just how he'd managed to fracture his wrist. Trying to dig out after he'd been pinned in and the snow had covered the opening to his dugout, he'd said.

She couldn't imagine the kind of panic that must have gone through him when the avalanche had covered his only way out, and he had no way of knowing if he was going to live. When he'd probably believed he was going to slowly suffocate to death before anyone could find him.

She shivered. She hated avalanches, even more so now that one had almost taken Stone away from her. She realized that she couldn't imagine her life without him.

And as she watched him being loaded into a life flight with the EMTs and the helicopter lifting away, she knew her heart was going with him.

Chapter Fifteen

Stone had managed to bust up his wrist and forearm pretty good, with broken bones in several places that were going to take a while to heal. He had a cast halfway up his arm. As far as he was concerned, those broken bones were his only real problem, but the doctors at the hospital refused to cut him loose even when he practically begged to go home. He was being held overnight for observation and was hooked up to an IV for fluids and had oxygen flowing through his nose.

He was itching to get out of his hospital bed and go find Felicity. One thing about meeting death head-on was the way it changed a man's perspective. There were the important things—the special people—and then there was the rest of life. He recalled his moments in the dugout before the avalanche, when he'd been admiring the claddagh ring he intended to give to Felicity.

Things had definitely changed in his heart and perspective on that count. He no longer wanted to offer her a promise ring. While it may have seemed like a good idea at the time, if almost dying had taught him one thing, it was that life was too short, and tomorrow wasn't promised. Likewise, he no longer felt he could make such a promise to her.

"Knock, knock." Felicity's sweet voice came from just outside the hospital door. "I've come to visit."

She came in backward, pushing the door open with her hip. Her hands were loaded with a huge bouquet of colorful early spring flowers and a bunch of Get Well Soon balloons. Under one elbow she carried a large card, probably half the size of her arm, and under the other the largest teddy bear he'd ever seen.

It was all he could do not to spring out of bed to help her, but he was still attached to an IV and wasn't going anywhere fast.

Then he heard a merry bark and the next moment Dandy was at his side, his front feet propped on the bed next to him, nosing under his palm and licking his knuckles.

"Hey, there, buddy. Well, look at you," Stone exclaimed. "How'd you get in here?"

"I couldn't come visit you without him," Felicity explained. "He was really missing you. It's a good thing for you he has an all-access hospital pass. Everybody around here knows him, so we didn't even get stopped in the hallway."

"Have you ever heard of overkill?" he teased as she looked for a place to put down the red glass vase bursting with blooms before tying the balloons to the foot of his bed. She put the teddy bear on a nearby chair.

"I just wanted you to be able to look around the room and remember that people care about you. I hope the balloons, flowers and Mr. Teddy will cheer you up a little bit. The last couple of days have been especially rough for you."

"*You* cheer me up," he insisted. "Thanks for stopping by."

"Oh," she said, sounding confused, and he realized he'd just made it sound like she should leave.

"I'm sorry," she said, patting his shoulder. "I'm sure you need to rest. I'll get out of here now."

"That's not what I meant at all," he scurried to tell her, grasping her arm with his good hand. "I really don't want you to leave."

She let out a breath. "Oh, good. I've been wanting to visit you ever since you were brought in on the life flight, but they told me I couldn't come see you until the next day. How are you feeling?"

"Like I ought to be able to go home. I'm fine. Other than this," he said, lifting his cast for her perusal, "there is absolutely no reason for them to keep me here. I've already stayed here overnight. As far as I'm concerned, that's enough observation for me."

"Doctors know best. You still have an IV and you're on oxygen. If they want to keep you another night or two, then be good and don't complain."

"Who, me? Complain?"

She rolled her eyes. "The nurses don't get paid enough to take care of you, I gather."

He grinned. "Hey, I've got a serious question for you."

Her gaze widened and he could tell she'd

stopped breathing. Her shoulders tightened perceptively.

Yeah, he'd said the wrong thing again, all right. Or at least, he'd said the right thing at the wrong time.

"My mama sent over pajamas and a change of clothes, but I didn't see my vest anywhere."

"I gave your cell phone to one of the EMTs on the life flight. Please don't tell me it didn't arrive at the hospital with you when you landed?"

Thoroughly flummoxed, he glanced at the tray next to him where he kept his cell phone. Why was she asking about his cell phone again?

"No. I mean yes. My cell phone is right there. The EMT made sure I got it when I was transferred to this room. That's not what I was asking about."

She shook her head. "What, then?"

"I was in shock and in a lot of pain when you pulled me out of that dugout, but I'm pretty sure I remember asking you to grab my vest."

"Well, yes, you did. Quite a few times, actually. But I thought that was because you were worried about your cell phone or you were in shock or something because of the panic and the pain."

"No, not my cell phone. But I do really, really need my vest."

"It's out in my car," she assured him, still appearing confused.

He let out a huge breath of air. "Thank you, Jesus. Would you mind going out and getting it for me?"

Though he knew she was confused, she agreed to run down and get his vest. He hoped she wouldn't get curious about his motives and look in any of the pockets. He almost told her not to but didn't want to get her curiosity up.

"Here you go," she said as she came back into the room with his vest in hand. "Why do you need it, again?"

He reached for it and as nonchalantly as possible felt around for the ring box. At first, he couldn't find it and his anxiety rose, but then he realized the vest was upside down and he was trying to feel inside the wrong pocket. He let out a deep breath.

"Come sit on the bed here," he said, pushing Dandy to the side and patting the space next to him, "and close your eyes."

She did as he bid, her hands clasped in her lap. "You're making me nervous, Stone," she said, laughing uneasily.

He chuckled. "If it makes you feel any better, I'm nervous, as well. Go ahead and open your eyes."

When she opened them, she stared down at the claddagh ring Stone now held in his hand.

"Oh," Felicity breathed, clapping a hand to her mouth. "I've never seen such a beautiful ring."

"I'm glad you like it. It's a claddagh ring."

"I love it."

He held her left hand in his but didn't immediately slide the ring on her finger.

"This ring has a lot of history behind it. It belonged to my mama, and then hers before her and so on all the way back to Ireland, where my family is from."

"That explains your mother's red hair," Felicity said with a smile.

"So, the reason why I volunteered so fast when they asked for someone to man the dugout was because I had this brilliant idea. I talked with the captain to tell him all about my plan and had him send you off in the right direction so you and Tugger would be the ones to find me. Then I was going to present this ring to you as a promise ring. I wanted to let you know my heart belongs to you and that I want to move forward in our relationship. I wanted to be exclusive. You and me."

"Oh, Stone." Felicity's beautiful blue eyes brimmed with tears. "That's so lovely."

"But I don't want to do that now," he continued.

"I—what?" Her face fell and he realized he'd just said the wrong thing.

Again.

"A claddagh ring serves many purposes. Inside are engraved the words *Friendship. Loyalty. Love.* I figure along with our faith in God, that describes exactly how I feel about you."

He smiled at her and continued, though it was awkward to hold her hand and the ring at the same time with his one good hand. But he wanted to make sure she understood what he was doing.

"On the right hand, heart inward, it's a promise ring. That's what I was originally intending to do. On the left hand, heart out, it's an engagement ring. And then the heart is turned inward on our wedding day."

Without another word, he slipped the ring on her left ring finger, heart outward.

"I— Are you—" she stammered.

"Asking you to marry me? Yes." He brought her hand to his lips and kissed the ring. "Believe it or not, I had time to think while I was buried in that avalanche, about how short life is and how we never know what each day is going to bring. I don't know where my life is taking me, but I am absolutely positive I want it to be here with you. I love you, Felicity. Will you be my wife?"

She stared at the ring for a long time, blinking back tears, and then she met his gaze and held it even longer.

"I feel the same way about you," she finally admitted. "When I thought I'd lost you, my heart broke in two. I couldn't imagine not having you in my life. I love you, too, Stone Keller, and it would be my very great blessing to become your wife."

His grin couldn't have been wider as he framed her face with his good hand and pulled her in for a kiss.

"I'm glad it could be just the two of us for this," he admitted. "But there are a lot of people who are going to want to hear about our future plans. My mama is going to be elated. I'm telling you right now, she's going to be cooking up wedding plans the second she hears about this."

"She's going to have to stand in line with my sisters. They can be incorrigible." She shifted until she was sitting on the bed next to Stone with her shoulder tucked under his.

"We'll have plenty of help."

"And I'm just warning you—my brothers may come at you with shotguns," she teased. "Just kidding. I'm certain they'll be just as happy for us as we are."

"Well, maybe not *quite* as happy," he said, leaning in for another kiss. "Because there's never been a man alive whose heart is as ecstatic as mine is right now. All I want to know is, how soon can we set the date? As far as I'm concerned, it can't be soon enough."

"I'd suggest we elope, but…"

"Those shotguns. Right."

She laid her head on his shoulder and sighed with happiness. He closed his eyes and savored the moment, inhaling the rose scent that was uniquely Felicity. He and Felicity were exactly where God wanted them to be.

* * *

Felicity stared at her ring, moving it back and forth in the light and admiring the way it sparkled. She couldn't have loved it more, though that was partly because of who'd given it to her. The heart was a green emerald surrounded by diamonds. The inside of the ring was engraved with the claddagh meaning, and indeed, the way she felt about the man she was going to marry.

Friendship. Loyalty. Love.

When she'd picked Stone up from the hospital, he was raring to go, anything to get away from being pinned down to a bed with an IV in his arm.

He wanted to tell the whole world they were engaged, and frankly, so did Felicity. She still had to pinch herself at times to realize such a good thing had come after what might have been the worst day of her life.

They'd decided to tell Stone's mother first before going to the farm and announcing their engagement to the whole Winslow clan. They found her curled up on her armchair with a crochet blanket over her. The TV was tuned to some home decorating channel, but she didn't appear to be watching it.

They thought she was dozing, and Stone tried to close the front door quietly, but her eyes popped open the moment they were inside.

"You're okay," she breathed, reaching out her hand to Stone. "I'm so glad. I couldn't go to the hospital because of my lowered immune system. I was so worried, and talking on the phone just wasn't good enough for me."

"I'm fine, Mama. I don't know why they made me stay in the hospital for two nights. There was nothing wrong with me other than my broken wrist. I hated every second of it."

"He's never been a good patient," Colleen told Felicity with a laugh. "Not from the time he was a little boy. You can imagine how he got when it came time for him to get his booster shots. He'd scream the moment we walked into the doctor's office."

He scoffed. "I still don't like shots. Or doctors."

Felicity pictured a little boy with Stone's red-gold hair and all-or-nothing attitude, and smiled. Stone had once used that mindset only to serve himself, but now those character traits served God. They made him an amazing man, and she would have the privilege of walking through life with him.

"Mama, we have something important to tell you." Stone reached for Felicity's left hand. "While I was stuck in the avalanche and then later in the hospital, I had a lot of time to think about how things went down. I'd originally planned to give her the ring as a promise ring, but at the end of the day, I couldn't imagine living without this woman, and she's consented to be my wife."

"Oh," said Colleen, breaking into tears. "I knew you two were perfect for each other from the first time Stone told me how he felt about you. I couldn't be happier for you."

"See?" Stone said. "I told you she'd like the news."

"We still have to tell all my siblings," Felicity explained. "My sisters will start writing out wedding invitations and planning the bridal shower, but my brothers may not take it as well as you have."

Colleen laughed. "I'm sure they won't. Any good brother would be protective of his sister. But if Stone is serious about you, and I know he is, he'll be able to take a little ribbing on your behalf."

They spent a few more minutes with Stone's mom talking over their engagement and how far out they wanted to plan their wedding. Stone wanted it sooner rather than later. So did Felicity, though she knew her family would insist on a big wedding that would take some time to plan.

While she'd felt entirely comfortable breaking the news to Colleen, she grew nervous as they drove back to the farm. What *would* Sharpe say about her marrying his best friend? It had been Sharpe's idea that they work together, after all, and it wasn't as if Stone had taken advantage of the situation.

They'd fallen in love with each other.

She called a family meeting to announce their engagement to everyone at once. All of her sisters' spouses and children were also present, curious as to what Felicity and Stone had to say.

"I have a huge announcement to make today. I have never been happier in my whole life," she prefaced her comments with a genuine smile. Most of her siblings echoed her smile with theirs, but Sharpe crossed his arms and narrowed his gaze.

"That's why I'm thrilled to tell you all that

Stone has asked me to marry him, and I said yes!" She held out her hand so her sisters could ooh and aah over her ring. Ruby's one-year-old son, Jayston, tried to put the ring in his mouth, while Jayston's twin sister, Moriah, sat on her daddy's knee clapping.

At least the children were happy for her.

"Congratulations," said Ruby, giving her a big hug. "I kind of thought there might be something going on between you two."

"Finally joining the ranks of us married ladies," Avery said, making it a three-way sister hug. "I hope our little surprise sleigh ride pushed you two in the right direction."

Felicity giggled. "Surprisingly, it did. I was mortified, but let's just say the night turned out well."

"We couldn't be happier for you," Molly said, wrapping her arms around Felicity and Avery and bringing the four sisters together, all of them in tears now. "And we get to plan another wedding!"

There were a series of groans from the nearby men, who all knew they'd be drawn into the planning whether they liked it or not.

"Stone, get in here," Molly demanded,

opening up a space for him to join in the group hug.

He laughed and joined in, his arms long enough to reach around all four of them.

After a minute, they finally split up. Felicity was well aware her brothers had not said anything about their engagement yet, and from the way Stone took her hand and gripped it tightly, he was aware of it, too.

Frost and Sharpe were standing shoulder to shoulder, both scowling and looking as intimidating as they could, arms crossed. Neither moved nor spoke as they stared at Felicity and Stone.

"Look, before you start in on me, you ought to know I love your sister with my whole heart," Stone said, his voice amazingly calm and forthright. "I asked her to marry me because I genuinely want to spend every day of the rest of my life caring for her, cherishing her, and making sure she knows just what a special woman she is."

Felicity's face was flaming at Stone's words, and she squeezed his hand to let him know she felt the same way about him. No matter what, she would be here standing beside him. Caring for him. Loving him and making sure he knew just how special he was.

"Well, then," Frost started, then paused.

"Looks to me as if no shotguns are necessary," Sharpe finished for him, stepping forward to bump shoulders with Stone in that manly hug they shared with each other. "Welcome to the family, brother. We're glad to have you."

Sharpe then whooped and twirled Felicity around. "Congrats, sis. You did good."

Frost also shoulder-bumped Stone and gave Felicity a bear hug. "God's blessings on you both," he whispered in her ear. "Stone's a good man."

"Well," said Avery's husband, Jake, his son on his shoulders, "Now that that's settled, I think we all need to celebrate."

"Who's for ice cream and cupcakes in town?" Ruby's husband, Aaron, asked, holding his daughter in his arms.

Everyone cheered and started getting in their cars to go to town.

"Ice cream and cupcakes?" Stone said in wonderment as they suddenly became the last ones heading for Whispering Pines. "I thought I'd be facing the chopping block, not chocolate chip cookie dough ice cream."

"I suppose you could say you were blessed," she suggested.

"Oh, I'm blessed, all right. No doubt about that. And I do want that chocolate chip cookie dough ice cream. But if we could just hang back here for just a second…"

He smiled and leaned down for the kiss that would seal their hearts forever.

Epilogue

Eighteen months later

In Felicity's family, it was hard to come up with a new way to do a gender reveal for a new baby. There had been so many already, and couples had been clever and creative in finding ways to announce their upcoming bundles of joy. Felicity especially remembered Aaron and Ruby. He had been the bearer of the big reveal and had baked a cupcake, which wasn't really all that new and unusual until Ruby bit into it and discovered purple cream in the middle.

Because pink and blue together made purple. She hadn't even known she was carrying twins until that day.

But now it was Felicity's turn, and she

was super excited to see what the family was going to do about it. She'd spent the first trimester of her pregnancy on the couch, as sick as a dog, and as far away from the smell and taste of food as Stone would allow her to go. He still made her eat, but he tenderly cooked whatever foods she thought she could stomach.

At least for Felicity, there was no such thing as morning sickness. It dragged on all day, every day, for weeks. She was just so grateful when she began to return to the land of the living.

And then she'd felt that first little movement. At first, she wasn't positive it was Baby Keller. It felt like butterflies loose in her womb. But it wasn't long before butterflies had become bumps, and she was looking forward to the time when she'd feel little heels kicking her ribs.

They had just finished their twenty-week ultrasound, and she had been amazed to see the precious baby on the screen. A little face. Sweet button nose. Two little hands. Kicking feet. It felt as if the baby was looking right at her, and she had squeezed Stone's hand so hard it must have hurt.

Ruby had come with them to the ultrasound, and she was the only one who'd been given the gender of Baby Keller from the ultrasound technician. She was absolutely thrilled to be the one to plan just how she wanted to reveal the baby's gender. Apparently, she had a creative idea in mind.

They got the whole family together in the Winslows' living room, including Stone's mother, who was now over one year cancerfree. She was looking well, and to her delight, her once-straight red hair had grown in curly.

"Okay, everyone, pipe down," Ruby said, holding up her hands for everyone to cease their conversations. "We're about to announce the news."

Felicity waited in anticipation.

A cake? A confetti popper? Balloons?

She looked around but didn't see anything out of the ordinary until Stone walked in with Dandy and Tugger all vested up and ready to work.

"We're going to have Felicity and Stone compete against each other," Ruby said with a laugh. "Stone, I know you've been in this family long enough to know we make everything into a friendly competition."

"Which I'm going to win," he said, winking at Felicity.

"You wish," she shot back. She might be carrying his child and have to walk a little more carefully, but she was still the best tracker in the family.

"Felicity and Tugger against Stone and Dandy," Ruby announced, as if it wasn't obvious who the teams would be.

"And we're looking for what?" Stone asked, clearly raring to get this game in gear. As usual, he looked as excited as his dog when it came to working as a team.

"I've buried one of Felicity's scarves somewhere out past the tree line behind the barn."

"How deep?" Stone queried. Felicity didn't care how deep. She had every faith in Tugger's ability to find and dig.

"I made it easy on you," Ruby assured him. "Ten inches. Both of your dogs can find well beyond that."

"I don't get it," Sharpe said, lifting his cowboy hat and scratching his head. "Why are they finding a scarf?"

The light went on in Felicity's mind even before Ruby could answer. "Because it will either be pink or blue."

Suddenly, she was just as excited as Stone appeared to be. Their eyes met and they shared a special smile. In just a few minutes they would know whether they were having a boy or a girl. Felicity honestly didn't care either way. It might be cliché, but all she wanted was a healthy baby. She would be equally excited for a boy or a girl, as would Stone.

"Let's go outside and we can get this race started," Ruby said. "I'm going to let these two teams go and then it's up to everyone else to keep up. I would say whichever team finds the scarf first wins, but I think in this case you'll both win."

Everyone went outside and Ruby lined the two teams up next to each other.

"Shouldn't Felicity get a head start?" Avery asked. "She's the one carrying the baby, after all."

Felicity shook her head. "Tugger and I don't need a head start. I can beat Stone fair and square."

"Okay, then," Ruby said. "Are you ready? Set? Go!"

Then they were off. Felicity quickly realized Stone did have a bit of an advantage in keeping up with his dog. Tugger was practically pulling her along because she had to step carefully. It was the middle of summer, but the gravel could still be slick under her feet.

Slow and steady wins the race, she told herself. She definitely felt like the turtle in this race. She walked like one. She laughed out loud at herself and concentrated on her dog.

"*Find*, Tugger," she commanded him, cutting out a different way than Stone had gone. She figured if the scarf was the direction he'd traveled, Dandy would have it dug out before she and Tugger could even get there. But if they were off by just a little…

Tugger suddenly alerted, barking steadily as he moved to the side.

They had it! Now all she had to do was get to it before Stone and Dandy.

Tugger was still pulling on his lead when she looked up and saw Stone and Dandy coming toward her from the other direction.

"Hurry," she told Tugger. *"Find."*

Tugger stopped just before Stone and Dandy reached them and started digging in the dirt. Felicity took out her shovel, but she looked up at Stone first.

He pulled Dandy back and gestured for her to go ahead.

"It's your win," he said with a grin.

She shook her head. "No. It's *our* win. I think we should do this together, don't you?"

"If you're sure."

"God blessed us both with this little one. Grab your shovel and let's see if we're going to be painting the nursery pink or blue."

The entire family gathered around them as the two teams dug, everyone chattering in anticipation and throwing out guesses as to what they would find.

Tugger and Dandy both picked up on the excitement and dug even faster, to the point where Stone and Felicity backed off to let their dogs do the hard labor.

Moments later, Tugger pulled up his prize.

A baby blue scarf.

They were having a boy. And Felicity hoped he would look just like his father, with red-gold hair and eyes so blue they reflected the sunlight.

Stone whooped and carefully grabbed her

by the waist, spinning her around as everyone cheered them on.

"We're going to have a son," Stone announced, as if the scarf hadn't already made that proclamation.

"Looks like," she said, framing his face and kissing his lips, something she never got tired of doing. "And I hope he looks just like his daddy."

"Don't wish that on the poor kid," Sharpe teased.

But she did wish. She wished it very much. And as Stone stood behind her, tucking her close to him, she pressed a palm to her belly, knowing she was the most blessed woman in the world.

* * * * *

Dear Reader,

I hope you are enjoying these tales—or should I say tails?—in the Rocky Mountain Family series. It was simply amazing to me in my research to discover the many and varied ways service dogs can be used. There aren't enough books in the world to cover them all!

In the book, pit bull mix Tugger and Dandy the black Labrador retriever work in disaster shelter therapy and avalanche search and rescue. Avalanches are Felicity's greatest fear, and the themes of conquering fears and walking through the dark night of the soul are front and center in this book, as they are in my own life right now—and, I suspect, the lives of many others.

This book features the fourth and last Winslow sister in my Rocky Mountain Family series, starring the six Winslow siblings who live and work on a Christmas tree farm as well as the service dog rescue center, A New Leash on Love, in the fictional town of Whispering Pines, Colorado.

I'm always delighted to hear from you,

dear readers, and I love to connect socially. To get regular updates, please visit my website and sign up for my newsletter at https://www.debkastnerbooks.com. Come join me on Facebook at *DebKastnerBooks,* and/or catch me on Twitter @debkastner.

Please know that I pray for each and every one of you without ceasing. When I sit down to write, it is with you in mind.

Dare to Dream,

Deb Kastner

HARLEQUIN SELECTS COLLECTION

19 FREE BOOKS IN ALL!

**From Robyn Carr to RaeAnne Thayne to
Linda Lael Miller and Sherryl Woods we promise
(actually, GUARANTEE!) each author in the
Harlequin Selects collection has seen their name on
the *New York Times* or *USA TODAY* bestseller lists!**

YES! Please send me the **Harlequin Selects Collection**. This collection begins with 3 FREE books and 2 FREE gifts in the first shipment. Along with my 3 free books, I'll also get 4 more books from the Harlequin Selects Collection, which I may either return and owe nothing or keep for the low price of $24.14 U.S./$28.82 CAN. each plus $2.99 U.S./$7.49 CAN. for shipping and handling per shipment*.If I decide to continue, I will get 6 or 7 more books (about once a month for 7 months) but will only need to pay for 4. That means 2 or 3 books in every shipment will be FREE! If I decide to keep the entire collection, I'll have paid for only 32 books because 19 were FREE! I understand that accepting the 3 free books and gifts places me under no obligation to buy anything. I can always return a shipment and cancel at any time. My free books and gifts are mine to keep no matter what I decide.

☐ 262 HCN 5576   ☐ 462 HCN 5576

Name (please print)

Address   Apt. #

City   State/Province   Zip/Postal Code

Mail to the **Harlequin Reader Service:**
IN U.S.A.: P.O. Box 1341, Buffalo, NY 14240-8531
IN CANADA: P.O. Box 603, Fort Erie, Ontario L2A 5X3

*Terms and prices subject to change without notice. Prices do not include sales taxes, which will be charged (if applicable) based on your state or country of residence. Canadian residents will be charged applicable taxes. Offer not valid in Quebec. All orders subject to approval. Credit or debit balances in a customer's account(s) may be offset by any other outstanding balance owed by or to the customer. Please allow 3 to 4 weeks for delivery. Offer available while quantities last. © 2020 Harlequin Enterprises ULC. ® and ™ are trademarks owned by Harlequin Enterprises ULC.

Your Privacy—Your information is being collected by Harlequin Enterprises ULC, operating as Harlequin Reader Service. To see how we collect and use this information visit https://corporate.harlequin.com/privacy-notice. From time to time we may also exchange your personal information with reputable third parties. If you wish to opt out of this sharing of your personal information, please visit www.readerservice.com/consumerschoice or call 1-800-873-8635. Notice to California Residents—Under California law, you have specific rights to control and access your data. For more information visit https://corporate.harlequin.com/california-privacy.

50BOOKHS22R

COMING NEXT MONTH FROM
Love Inspired

THEIR SECRET COURTSHIP
by Emma Miller
Resisting pressure from her mother to marry, Bay Stutzman is determined to keep her life exactly as it is. Until Mennonite David Jansen accidentally runs her wagon off the road. Now Bay must decide whether sharing a life with David is worth leaving behind everything she's ever known...

CARING FOR HER AMISH FAMILY
The Amish of New Hope • by Carrie Lighte
Forced to move into a dilapidated old house when entrusted with caring for her *Englisch* nephew, Amish apron maker Anke Bachman must turn to newcomer Josiah Mast for help with repairs. Afraid of being judged by his new community, Josiah tries to distance himself from the pair but can't stop his feelings from blossoming...

FINDING HER WAY BACK
K-9 Companions • by Lisa Carter
After a tragic event leaves widower Detective Rob Melbourne injured and his little girl emotionally scarred, he enlists the services of therapy dog handler Juliet Newkirk and her dog, Moose. But will working with the woman he once loved prove to be a distraction for Rob...or the second chance his family needs?

THE REBEL'S RETURN
The Ranchers of Gabriel Bend • by Myra Johnson
When a family injury calls him home to Gabriel Bend, Samuel Navarro shocks everyone by arriving with a baby in tow. His childhood love, Joella James, reluctantly agrees to babysit his infant daughter. But can she forget their tangled past and discover a future with this newly devoted father?

AN ORPHAN'S HOPE
by Christina Miller
Twice left at the altar, preacher Jase Armstrong avoids commitment at all costs—until he inherits his cousin's three-day-old baby. Pushing him further out of his comfort zone is nurse Erin Tucker and her lessons on caring for an infant. But can Erin convince him he's worthy of being a father *and* a husband?

HER SMALL-TOWN REFUGE
by Jennifer Slattery
Seeking a fresh start, Stephanie Thornton and her daughter head to Sage Creek. But when the veterinary clinic where she works is robbed, all evidence points to Stephanie. Proving her innocence to her boss, Caden Stoughton, might lead to the new life she's been searching for...

LOOK FOR THESE AND OTHER LOVE INSPIRED BOOKS WHEREVER BOOKS ARE SOLD, INCLUDING MOST BOOKSTORES, SUPERMARKETS, DISCOUNT STORES AND DRUGSTORES.

LICNM0122A